George Graham Currie

How I Once Felt : Songs of love and Travel

George Graham Currie

**How I Once Felt : Songs of love and Travel**

ISBN/EAN: 9783744767262

Printed in Europe, USA, Canada, Australia, Japan

Cover: Foto ©Andreas Hilbeck / pixelio.de

More available books at **www.hansebooks.com**

# SONGS OF LOVE

AND

# TRAVEL

BY

GEO. G. CURRIE.

---

MONTREAL:

JOHN LOVELL & SON, PRINTERS.

1893.

DEDICATED

TO THE

# BURRARD LITERARY SOCIETY,

OF

VANCOUVER, B.C.,

AND TO

# THE ROSCOE CLUB,

OF

MONTREAL, P.Q.,

IN MEMORY OF MANY HAPPY HOURS SPENT WITHIN THE
CONFINES OF THEIR FAVORED CIRCLES.

# PREFACE.

In presenting the following compositions to my literary friends and to the Canadian public in general, I do so with the honest hope that I am contributing to their amusement and edification.

The poems, however, were not originally intended for publication ; indeed, they have already doubly served the purpose for which they were designed, since by their aid I have not only whiled away many a leisure moment, or won the closer friendship of persons whose confidence I most desired, but have gained—what to the poet's fancy is a breath from heaven and pre-eminently man's greatest boon—the smiles and perhaps dearer favors of the fairer sex.

I do not attempt to claim perfection of either sentiment or versification for any of my trifles. Each particular production is the effect of some particular experience, and being written as many were on the spur of some fleeting moment, it will surely be excusable in me to say that I have outgrown the enthusiasm or callousness which some of them represent.

6
*PREFACE.*

This therefore is my apology for calling the collection by the
very non-committal appellation of " How I Once Felt."

A desire to test the market value of my only stock in trade,
combined with the advice of possibly prejudiced friends,
some time ago set me thinking of the present step; but, loth
to risk being the object of ignorant ridicule or the financial
loser in case of failure to interest, I have been slow—very
slow—in summoning up the necessary courage.

Scott's inspiriting verse,

> " He either fears his fate too much,
> Or his deserts are small,
> Who dares not put it to the touch,
> To win or lose it all,"

has finally steeled me to the effort ; and I now launch my
little boat upon the waves of public opinion.  If its cargo is
dead weight, then let it sink as it ought into oblivion ; but, on
the other hand, should there be even one spark of life to guide
and keep it safe through its pilgrimage and buffetings, there
will be at least one anxious pair of eyes following its progress
to the longed-for goal, and that pair I need hardly say will
belong to

Yours very sincerely,

THE AUTHOR.

# INDEX.

## POEMS.

# SONGS OF TRAVEL, ETC.

# TO MY MUSE.

Sweet Poesy, thou nymph divine,—
  My dearest hope and pride ;
My heart now offers at thy shrine
  The debt it cannot hide.

When to thy coy and countless charms
  My musing mem'ry strays,
My spirit with the contact warms,
  And I am filled with praise.

In sorrow thou art ever nigh,
  My mournful hours to cheer ;
In happiness, wert thou not by,
  'Twould make my bliss less dear.

When Friendship calls for tribute just,
  Or Cupid claims his due,
Thou never yet betrayed my trust,—
  Thy help is sure and true.

Here let me own with grateful grace,
  Thou art my only guide ;
With thee—what matters time or place ;
  Without—e'en heaven is void.

# CANADA.

Oh Canada, the fairest child
  Of Britain old and strong;
Of thee we think, of thee we speak,
  Of thee shall be our song.
Thy land so fertile and so vast
  Reaches from sea to sea;
Thy lakes and rivers, unsurpas't,
  Are emblems of the free.

Thy mountains, sloping gracefully,
  High up in air do rise;
Their snow cap't tops amid the clouds,
  Are hidden from our eyes.
Thy woodlands bloom with lordly pines,
  And maples fresh and green.
Thy valleys, cover'd o'er with grain,
  Are smiling with its sheen.

Thy sons, so brave and true, have shown
  Of what their hearts are made,
By rising quickly to thy call,
  Rebellion to degrade.
Thy daughters, too, so pure and sweet,
  With health and beauty blest,
Reveal thy charms and sing thy praise
  With true Canadian zest.

May Peace, Prosperity and Power,
  Be thine for evermore;
May staunch Integrity, thy dower,
  Be known from shore to shore:
May thy good name ne'er tarnish'd be
  By tyrant's cruel hand:
This, Canada, we wish for thee,
  Our home and native land.

B

## VERSES.

(Composed after reading Emerson's essay on " The Oversoul. ")

What a pleasure there's in knowing
   I'm a part of God's great plan ;
What a priv'lege then in doing
   All for Him I truly can.

What a balm there's in the knowledge
   That what I sincerely do,
Is His Spirit working in me,
   And, confined, comes bursting through.

Just to think that through each action
   Born of this—my warring frame,
He, the great undimmed attraction,
   Speaks, my brothers to reclaim.

That same God we see in mountains,
   In the plains and mighty sea,
In great rivers, bubbling fountains,
   In the flowers,—is seen in me.

When grim Passion tears my vitals,
   And I fight it to the death ;
'Tis not me, but God that conquers,
   Me it was that gave up breath.

And whene'er I work in earnest,
   And my deeds with glory shine,
Thou, Most High, my power adornest ;
   With Thy help I'm made|divine.

Give me then, oh Great Creator,
   Greater power with flesh to cope ;
Let me tear aside its hindrance,
   To give Thee more light, more scope.

Wondrous theme, Great Soul of Nature,
  In Thy praise I'm filled with song ;
I, a mortal wayward creature,
  Still to Thee, in Thee belong.

------

## WHAT IS LOVE?

Love is the secret of success,
In it alone lies happiness :
No lover ever loved in vain :
A mistress lost was equal gain.
The martyr died that he might live ;
His very death new life can give :
For love of truth he singly bled
And is, by life immortal, paid.
The patriot's tomb is hallowed still ;
He died, but 'gainst his country's will ;
He loved his home, and in return
Men worship now his storied urn.
The poet,—who? what made him such?
When truth is known 'twas loving much ;
The prophet, too, and famous king,
Are fam'd because of love they bring.
But doubt you still, I then contend,
'Tis love that constitutes a friend ;
Man's dearest boon, his greatest joy,
The bliss that knows no base alloy.
Why, then, my brother, your delay
In letting out this heav'nly ray ?
Inquire not where it can be found,
But raise your eyes and look around.
Why think you shines the sun on high ?
Why flit those clouds across the sky ?
Is it for naught the brooklets run ?

Do mighty rivers flow for fun ?
What motive caused the flowers to spring ?
And with the bud why perfume bring ?
Is there no good in fen and brake ?
Are landscape views a grand mistake ?
What draws us to the mountain wild ?
Why rocks in massive grandeur piled ?
What makes the great Niag'ra roar,
While luscious fruits grow by its shore ?
Were pretty birds whose songs so thrill
But made for beasts and sports to kill ?
No, God be praised, the reason's plain :
'Twas love in our Creator's brain ;
And love in Him means love in us,
We're part of Him, He's all of us.
Shake off the cloak ! let shine your light !
Why 'gainst your inner nature fight ?
As bright as are those stars above
Is seen in you this wonder—Love.

---

## OLD IRELAND FOREVER.

(Written for my Irish friends, R. J. H. and J.A.M.)

Though Burns and Scott with poets' skill
Have famous made each Scottish rill ;
Though Hogg makes many a bosom thrill,
I must confess I'm Irish still.

Though England, with unwonted zeal,
To Shakespeare's genius may appeal ;
Though she may proud of Dickens feel,
I love the land of Swift and Steele.

Though Frenchmen laugh at Molière's mirth,
Or read of Hugo round their hearth :

*Yours ever John A. Milligan*

Though Germans talk of Gœthe's worth,
I'm from the land of Goldsmith's birth.

Though Yankees, with a patriot smile,
May praise Longfellow's winning style,
Or talk of Irving all the while,
I'd fain have Moore my hours beguile.

Though poets near and far abroad
Their home and country well may laud,
I still with fervor pray that God
Will bless my own dear Erin's sod.

---

## VERSES IN MEMORY OF J. A. MILLIGAN.

(Who, with five others, was drowned in the St. Lawrence river, near
Montreal, July 2nd, 1892.)

I had a boon companion, a tried and trusty friend ;
    Together we had played when we were boys ;
Together had we rambled, nor recked that youth must end,
    And with it all its dearest cherished joys.

His smile was all I wished for to crown a boyish feat ;
    To him I told whatever went amiss :
Our secret thoughts were common, nor were our hopes
        complete
    Without each being party to their bliss.

But time is ever fleeting ; no longer did we play
    The games that had beguiled each childish hour ;
And as we grew to manhood with ev'ry passing day,
    Our boy love gained intensity and power.

I gloried in his friendship—the purest gift on earth ;
    I felt that he was noble and sincere ;
I proudly called him comrade, and recognized his worth
    In striving by his life my own to steer.

But best of friends are parted—ambition cut the tie ;
    I left him, travelled honors fain to earn :
And being young and sanguine I scarcely heaved a sigh,
    Anticipating soon a sweet return.

Three summers slowly faded, and still from him apart,
    My phantom fortune held me far away :
But mem'ry's tender missives kept warm within my heart
    A corner where that friend had perfect sway.

Then hopes grew bright and brighter—good times were draw-
            ing near :
    Soon back to him and home I would be bound ;
When suddenly a message made life a prospect drear :
    *The comrade of my boyhood had been drowned.*

That brave and boon companion, that tried and trusty friend
    Had rudely from expectant plans been torn,
To cross that mystic portal where pain and pinings end ;
    While I, alas ! am left to live and mourn.

So now, alone, dejected, a void within my breast,
    Impatiently I do my doubtful part ;
The pleasures that I long for are pleasures of the past,
    And naught but death can soothe my aching heart.

## NATURE'S COMFORTERS.

Babies, and music, and flowers ;—
    Tokens of infinite love—
Coming like soft summer showers,
    Fresh from the heavens above :
These, in our moments of sadness,
    Temper our sorrows with joy,
Fill our lone hearts with their gladness,
    Banish all baneful alloy.

Violets, lilies and roses—
    Emblems of virtue and truth ;
Sweet-smelling, blossoming posies,
    Buds of perpetual youth :
All give us proof of perfection,
    Promise of provident powers ;
Mutely compel our subjection
    To beautiful, billowy flowers.

Touches of ecstatic passion ;
    Whispered suggestions of woe ;
Breathings of coming elation ;
    Mem'ries of long, long ago :
These into harmony blended,
    Aided by angelic art,
Lighten the loads that offended,
    Melt e'en the stoniest heart.

Innocent, infantile charmers,—
    Flowers and music combined,—
Smiling faced, dimpled disarmers,
    Ruling both matter and mind :
Plucked from the meadows of heaven ;
    Cooing in melody sweet ;
These are (in tenderness given)
    God's antidote for deceit.

Babies, and music, and flowers, —
    Tokens of infinite love—
Coming like soft, summer showers,
    Fresh from the heavens above :
These, in our moments of sadness,
    Temper our sorrows with joy,
Fill our lone hearts with their gladness,
    Banish all baneful alloy.

## THE " BEAVER."

On some rocks near the entrance to Burrard Inlet, B.C., lies all that remains of the " Beaver," the pioneer steamer of our Western coast. Natur- ally enough, considering her age, she was not a vessel of very large ton- nage ; while her machinery and accommodation, though a marvel at the time of construction, are to a modern eye of the very rudest description. Notwithstanding these facts, however, the old fossil may very justly be termed the fore-runner of civilization in British Columbia, for prior to her appearance, the valley of the Fraser and the province generally for that matter, was the haunt only of bears and of Indians.

Beside Trade's brisk and busy way,
    The Beaver stranded lies ;
Her storied timbers, ocean's prey,
    Or greedy vandal's prize.
Her days of usefulness gone by,
    Upon her rocky bed,
She starts and strains with creak and sigh,
    To find her glory fled.

The world moves on with thankless jeer,
    Nor calls to mind the day
When round Cape Horn, with welcome cheer,
    She steamed her maiden way.
Pacific's pioneer she faced
    To conquer ev'ry " how ?"
And dauntlessly through unknown waste
    Pushed firm her sturdy prow.

From Golden Gate to Cariboo,
    Each miner owned her fame ;
And loudly when she hove in view,
    Sent heavenward her name :
From far-off climes she brought them news,
    While stored within her hold,
Were comforts that could re-enthuse
    Tired searchers after gold.

PIONEER STEAMER "BEAVER" AND C.P.R. ROYAL MAIL STEAMER "EMPRESS OF INDIA."
OFF OBSERVATION POINT, VANCOUVER, B.C.

She came the harbinger of good,
　　While virgin forests bowed ,
But what she brought in hopeful mood
　　Has long since proved her shroud.
Her coming loosed a mighty wheel,
　　Which, slowly turning round,
Has crushed her hopes with heartless zeal,
　　Nor uttered pitying sound.

But, dear old Beaver, never fear,
　　Your friends are not all dead ;
I've often through the starting tear
　　Surveyed your cheerless bed.
And though your usefulness is past,—
　　Your days of triumph o'er,
So long as life in verse can last,
　　Will live your feats of yore.

---

## A POET'S PLIGHT.

This poem is the recollection of an experience which I once went through near Portland, Ore. It was undoubtedly a punishment meted out by Providence for a more than ordinarily glaring lack of foresight.

The friends referred to in the last verse are Ben. E. and John S. Lyster then of Coos County, Oregon, and formerly of Richmond, Que., Canada.

Broke ! Broke ! Broke !
　　Was the lot of a wandering bard ;
Broke ! Broke ! Broke !
　　In a city where nobody cared ;
Broke ! Broke ! Broke !
　　And in misery, hunger and rags,
He tried hard to get work,
The dishonor to shirk
　　Of his being imprisoned with " vags."

Hope ! Hope ! Hope !
  Could he only get out of the town ;
Hope ! Hope ! Hope !
  He might then escape poverty's frown ;
Hope ! Hope ! Hope !
  But how best was the thing to be done ?
He must certainly walk,
For his long-hoarded stock
  To the drainings was now nearly run.

Tramp ! Tramp ! Tramp !
  Without e'en a change to his back ;
Tramp ! Tramp ! Tramp !
  O'er the ties of a hard, stony track ;
Tramp ! Tramp ! Tramp !
  Till his old clothes began to wear out ;
Then with feet almost bare,
And with husks for his fare,
  Highest hopes were soon turned into doubt.

Tired ! Tired ! Tired !
  As he counted the ties on his way ;
Tired ! Tired ! Tired !
  Still he plodded along, day by day ;
Tired ! Tired ! Tired !
  And as weeks followed others along,
Was it wonder he sighed
O'er the grave of his pride ?
  Or that plaintive and sad was his song ?

Sleep ! Sleep ! Sleep !
  Would he ever again know its bliss ?
Sleep ! Sleep ! Sleep !
  What misdeed had he sown to reap this ?
Sleep ! Sleep ! Sleep !

How it mocked through the long, dreary night ;
As with straw for a bed,
In some dark dingy shed,
  He lay cursing grim fate for his plight.


Dreams ! Dreams! Dreams !
  Of the pleasures he knew in the past ;
Dreams ! Dreams ! Dreams !
  O'er his troubles a halo they cast ;
Dreams ! Dreams ! Dreams !
  But alas ! they were fitful and brief ;
And but served, while awake,
Greater contrasts to make ;
  Thus adding more fuel to his grief.


Sick ! Sick ! Sick !
  For misfortunes ne'er singly do come ;
Sick ! Sick ! Sick !
  Lying thousands of miles from his home ;
Sick ! Sick ! Sick !
  Thickly covered with vermin and rags.
May the horrors he knew
Be the lot of but few,
  As he moaned on his pillow of bags.


Bread ! Bread ! Bread !
  Once again he must take to the road ;
Bread ! Bread ! Bread !
  With fell Hunger his leader and goad ;
Bread ! Bread ! Bread !
  But the people were deaf to his wants--
He was only a tramp,
And most likely a scamp—
  So they answered his pleadings with taunts.

Friends ! Friends ! Friends !
  After long weeks of tramping had passed ;
Friends ! Friends ! Friends !
  The poor poet found favor at last ;
Friends ! Friends ! Friends !
  Who generously gave him a start ;
And a song in whose praise,
To the end of his days,
  He will sing from the depths of his heart.

---

## VANCOUVER.

(A parody on Longfellow's ",Excelsior.)

The summer's sun was waning low
Behind a western hillock's brow ;
As, by a little pamphlet caught,
An Eastern youth first grasped the thought,—
           " Vancouver."

As if by instinct forth he drew
His purse, and searched it through and through ;
And as enough he there espied
To pay his way, he loudly cried,—
           ' Vancouver."

"What ! What is that ? " the old man said,
" You are not fit to earn your bread."
He turned, and fire flashed from his eye,
As half suppressed all heard this cry,—
           " Vancouver."

His many friends gave kind advice,
And from his purpose to entice
Tried ev'ry means they could conceive ;
But with this word he took his leave,—
           " Vancouver."

"O, do not go!" fair Delia sighed,
With look that would a god have tried;
But true unto his purpose still,
He answered back, in accents shrill,—
                          " Vancouver."

Great cities smiled to take him in
As on his way he heard their din ;
 But on their flatt'ring smiles he frowned,
And in this shriek their din was drowned,—
                          " Vancouver."

Across the prairie wild and wide,
His onward course he daily hied ;
Though shot on shot he saw at game,
His course and song was still the same,—
                          " Vancouver."

The Rocky mountains soon at hand,
He scaled their heights not yet unmanned ;
And clambered over cliff and ford,
Repeating oft the self-same word—
                          " Vancouver."

Through gorge and canyon lies his way,
His strength—not spirit—fails each day ;
For nothing daunted, on he hies,
And echoes answer from the skies,—
                          " Vancouver."

At last a wreck he sights the town;
The natives greet him with a frown :
Too great the shock, he forward falls,
But dying, still that cry recalls,—
                          " Vancouver."

And now he lies unwept, unsung,
The scarred and straggling stumps among ;
While not far from the unhonored dead
Goes on with brisk and busy tread,—
                          " Vancouver."

## FELINE PHILOSOPHY.

I was musing one day in the old-fashioned way,
    Trying hard to commune with my fate ;
While' side me there sat a purring old cat,
    In a quiet and dignified state :
" What " says I, while stroking my feline friend's coat,
    " Is the acme of all that is nice ? "
When, judge my surprise as from pussy's black throat,
    Came the answer quite audibly—" mice."

Dear, dear ! how absurd ! thought I with a smile ;
    I must surely be dreaming to-day ;
A cat cannot talk ; to think so is vile !
    And puss purred her monotonous lay :
Then in rev'rie again,"Is there nought to attain,
    Without 'gaging worlds in our spats ? "
When distinct as before, from her seat on the floor,
    Grimalkin looked up and said " rats."

## ONLY A SIWASH DOG.

While on a canoe trip from Juneau, Alaska, to the Skeena River, B.C.
my companion and I were surprised one morning by the appearance at our
camp of a half-starved Eskimo (or Siwash) dog.   We were probably one
hundred miles from any village or settlement at the time, and of this fact our
canine visitor seemed fully aware. It had probably been forgotten on shore
by some wandering party of Indians, and coming across our track had con-
cluded that its one last hope for life lay in our generosity. Not being over-
stocked with provisions, and being unable to tell within two or three days'
voyage of our distance from the nearest supply place, we could ill afford the
animal a meal.   Grateful for what little we did spare, the dog kept our
canoe in sight all morning, and when we finally started across the mouth
of an inlet—at least four miles across—the poor brute recognized its predicament, and for hours its howls of misery, human almost in their pathos,
were wafted over the water as we glided away.   It was at least two days

after the incident, but while the sound was still ringing in my ears, that being detained on shore by stress of weather I wrote the verses which follow :—

Only a Siwash dog, gaunt, ugly and lean ;
Too currish to run, yet ashamed to be seen ;
Yellow and stunted, of famine the mark ;
Worthless, excepting to eat and to bark ;
Deserted on shore by its master and friends,
With a shy, furtive look to our camp it descends.

Alone in Alaska ! Bleak, barren and wild,
Where mountains of rock on each other are piled ;
Alone on a strand where encampments are few,
Where mankind is scarce, and where dogkind is, too ;
Where food is so precious that none could we spare
From our hampers already harassingly bare.

Only a Siwash dog, gaunt, ugly and all ;
What does it matter ?   Its earnings are small.
Still, as I gaze on its keen, wistful eye,
As it sniffs out the place where our provisions lie,
My heart gives a twitch, and its hunger I feel,
Till I hasten to give it the ghost of a meal.

At length we embark and row out from the bay,
While the dog follows hard on the beach half a day ;
But woe to his hopes ! for a crossing we make
That leaves him a prisoner far in our wake.
Out he stands on a point jutting into the sea,
And howl after howl shows his deep misery.

Only a Siwash dog, gaunt, ugly and lean ;
Does it matter at all what his ending has been ?
Perhaps not ; but still as I wander through life,
And gaze on its sorrows, its cares and its strife,
All cries of misfortune will call to my ear
That Siwash dog's howls as we left him so drear.

## A SPEECH.

(Supposed to be made at the opening of Lindsay Collegiate Institute,
Jan. 25th, 1889.)

I do not wish with long oration,
And weighty tedious demonstration,
To make you, by your yawns, betray
Fatigue on this our natal day ;
Nor do I, with a pompous style,
Intend to cause an inward smile ;
For by your looks and silent nudges,
I fear, alas ! you're able judges ;
So, if you've no applause to spare,
Pray with my feeble efforts bear.
Just listen, and appear at ease—
For know, kind friends, I wish to please.

There was a time in ages past
When learning was a stigma cast
By people, on those favored few,
Who, seeking wisdom, waded through
The musty depths of learned lore
That sages wrote in books of yore ;
But later on as time progressed,
And evolution ne'er at rest
Caused civ'lization to advance,
And gave the vulgar crowd a chance
To taste the sweets in learning's train,
And showed the heights they might attain.
A wondrous change at length took place ;
And those, who once with sneering face
Had laughed to scorn the few who tried
To pluck the fruit to fools denied,
Became as eager to devise
A means by which they too might rise ;

Content no longer to be fools,
They built them colleges and schools
Wherein their off-spring might be taught
The truths which they themselves had not.

But still they scarce conceived their worth ;
Of knowledge yet there was a dearth.
Their colleges were far from good ;
The schools they built were plain and rude ;
They let them fall into decay,—
Nor raised a hand Time's rage to stay—
Till plaster from the ceilings fell ;
The walls by cracks their age could tell ;
And windows with their lights half gone
Had used up copies fastened on ;
Displaying both the pupils' drift
And parents' economic thrift ;
And he who failed to be of use
In other callings more abstruse
Was straightway hired with task assigned
To rear and train the youthful mind.

Yet lo ! with never tiring tread
Fast onward evolution sped ;
And now to-day with conscious pride
We point you to its wondrous stride ;
An ample proof, this building stands,
The work of well skilled artists' hands ;
No proven comfort does it lack,
A model school from front to back ;—
A palace 'tis—to call it less
We would the law of truth transgress.
Each class-room like a parlor made
Incites our youth to mount that grade—
(So rough and steep as sages claim)—
Which leads to knowledge and to fame.

The school in which we now are met
For building may you ne'er regret;
Though it has been a heavy strain,
And has to many seemed a bane,
Yet here it stands a monument
Of all the time and means you've spent.
Its pupils all and each your debtor
Confess they wish for nothing better.
And now, proved friends of education,
Before I close this dedication:
For all your previous thoughtful aid
To make this building as 'tis made ;
And also here I beg to mention
For present patient kind attention,
Accept my thanks, and those to boot
Of Lindsay Collegiate Institute.

---

## WHAT THE BELLBUOY SAYS.

Near the entrance to San Diego harbor, Cal., there is a large buoy with a fog bell on top, to warn sailors of their proximity to dangerous shoals.

Far out on the surf of a rockbound coast,
　The bellbuoy lonely tolls,
And utters its wierd, uncanny boast
　O'er the deep's uncounted ghouls.
It rises and falls with the restless tide,—
　No sea can immerse its song ;
The wind and the wave alike defied,
　But strengthen its dong ding dong.
　　　Tolling, tolling, patiently tolling,
　　　Over the billows swelling and rolling,
　　　Dong ding dong, dong ding dong,
　　　Look to your helm, your course is wrong ;
　　　Dong ding dong, ding dong, ding dong,
　　　This is the bellbuoy's lonely song.

Many a mariner shrouded in fog —
    Feeling his doubtful way—
Relies to his cost on compass and log,
    Till warned by that timely lay.
We too might be warned as we enter the mist
    On Life's beclouded main,
For a voice in our bosom, if we but list,
    Is singing the self-same strain.
        Tolling, tolling, patiently tolling
        Over Life's billows swelling and rolling,
        Dong ding dong, dong ding dong,
        Look to your helm, your course is wrong ;
        Dong ding dong, ding dong, ding dong,
        This too is conscience's whispered song.

## WASHINGTON'S BIRTHDAY.

While sojourning in Juneau, Alaska, early in the year 1890, I obtained, by various means, some little reputation for the making of bad poetry, and a Presbyterian divine (Rev. S. H. King), struggling hard to place Christianity in a popular light before the inhabitants of that out-of-the-way corner of the world, surprised me one day by inviting me to read an original poem at a service he proposed holding on the 22nd of February (Washington's Birthday). I naturally felt somewhat diffident about accepting such an invitation, and contended amongst other things that, being a Canadian, it would hardly be appropriate for me (to say the least) to stand up and eulogize a person who, hero or no hero, must in the eyes of many of my own countrymen be and ever remain a rebel. By the use of judicious praise, however, and a little flattery, I was finally persuaded, and at the appointed time, after explaining to the audience my peculiar predicament, I told them that the following verses were what I might have felt, had not my lucky star located my birth-place twenty-five miles north of the U.S. boundary.

Washington's birthday ! Hark, hark to the sound
    Of joy universal and glee ;
Washington's birthday ! Still let it resound,
    With praises and proud jubilee ;

Washington's birthday! Oh why are we thrilled?
　　Oh why do we hallow the name?
Because since that day our hearts have been filled
　　With that which puts tyrants to shame.

Though eighteen decades are now nearly o'er—
　　A year has but to go by—
Since Washington's birth,—yet all men adore
　　A name that sure cannot die.
The world as it speeds its bustling career
　　In progress and civilization,
Pauses to honor the day it holds dear,—
　　That day so much prized by our nation.

Washington's birthday! What funds of delight
　　Those words have power to recall;
The champion of freedom, justice and right
　　Then came our hearts to enthrall.
Sing loudly, ye patriots, shout out your joy,
　　Commemorate liberty's birth;
Let cheers of rejoicing—with nought to alloy—
　　Awake and encompass the earth.

May the star-spangled banner he fought for so well
　　Still wave o'er a land for the free;
May the virtues he practised through our actions tell
　　That virtue is freedom's best plea;
May Columbia's strand which he loved and revered,
　　Still echo with song and applause
For the hero, who, father of all that he reared,
　　Gave us freedom and country and laws.

## THE BOARDIN' MISSIS' SMILE.

Though I've been in many lands,
And have passed through many hands,
In my search for peace and comfort without guile ;
Yet I have found out at last,
That all joy in life is past,
If you cannot make your boardin' missis smile.

Though your friends be of the best,
And you sport a satin vest,
And at balls and picnics live in highest style ;
All your pomp will be in vain,
For no real joy can you gain
If you cannot make your boardin' missis smile.

When your wages are increased—
Say five hundred at the least,
It may make you feel quite happy for a while ;
But it is not worth a song
(Though, of course, I may be wrong)
If you cannot make your boardin' missis smile.

If some little Cupid's dart
Has with love inflamed your heart,
And your lady takes it off into exile ;
While you wait your wedding morn,
You will wish you ne'er was born
If you cannot make your boardin' missis smile.

If a bachelor you stay,
And you hoard your cash away,
Till at length you have contrived to save a pile ;
What is all your money worth,
Is it use for aught on earth
If you cannot make your boardin' missis smile ?

So, young man just starting out,
　　Take advice, and you, no doubt,
Will ensure yourself real comfort by this wile ;
　　If with you the girls do flirt,
　　Treat them kind, but be alert
That you always court the boardin' missis' smile.

---

## HE COULDN'T SIT DOWN.

One day I determined to go for a ride,—
　　Though 'twas long since I'd mounted a horse,—
And felt so indignant, it injured my pride,
　　When told I'd be sorry—or worse.
I grew quite impatient at every delay
　　While waiting to saddle " the brown " ;
And until the hostler was well on the way,
　　I couldn't be made to sit down.

*Chorus.*—I couldn't sit down, I couldn't sit down,
　　　　No, I really couldn't sit down ;
　　　　You may laugh if you please,
　　　　You may titter and tease ;
　　　　But I really couldn't sit down.

As soon as my steed was in trim for the road,
　　I strove to get onto his back ;
But though I quite loudly and earnestly " whoaed,"
　　He wouldn't stand still in his track.
Undaunted I smiled at the gathering throng,
　　To show them I was not a clown ;
But with one stirrup short and the other one long,—
　　I really couldn't sit down.

　　　　　　　*Chorus.*

In time I was able to manage the beast,
   And flew from the place like a shot ;
Says I to myself, " Now I'm in for a feast,
   And one I'll remember, I wot."
I tried to ride easy and practised the lope ;
   But 'twould make e'en a Methodist frown,—
That horse and that saddle so jolted me up,
   That I didn't know how to sit down.
           *Chorus.*

At last when I thought I would surely succumb,
   And my body seemed limp as a rag,
I once more got back to the " pleasures of home,"
   And off from that dastardly nag.
But my troubles alas ! did not end with the ride,
   And I soon was the laugh of the town,
For no matter how tenderly careful I tried,—
   For a fortnight I could not sit down.
           *Chorus.*

---

## HOW HE WAS CURED.

There was once a little fellow
  Who was noted over town
For the way in which he used to brag and boast ;
  Though his brain was very shallow
  Yet he strutted up and down
And could talk a negro pale as Hamlet's ghost.
  But this tedious little vaunter
  Had a lesson yet to learn,
Of the which he hadn't even got the key,
  For while out upon a saunter
  To the wharf he chanced to turn,
Where it struck him that he'd like to go to sea.

So this dapper little boaster
  Who was sure he knew it all,

Made enquiries " What is due to leave the bay ? "
    And on being shown a coaster,
  In a tone that might appal,
He desired " to buy a stateroom right away."
    Soon the vessel weighed her anchor,
  O'er the billows steamed her course,
And at once began to toss and pitch and roll ;
    Then our hero's face grew blanker,
  And his voice was faintly hoarse
As he asked " what time the steamer reached its goal? "

    It was not so much the ocean,
  Or the breaker's foaming tops,
That made our talking friend become so meek ;
    It was more the sinking motion,
  As the vessel downward drops,
That caused the knowing blood to leave his cheek.
    He could stand the windy weather,
  Or the whitecaps on the sea,
The swells were terrors only to a clown ;
    But they could not harm a feather,
  And to him but toys would be,
If that vessel could be kept from coming down.

    When at last a port was sighted,
  He was overwhelmed with joy,
Though it was not where he was supposed to land ;
    And among the first who 'lighted
  Was this cured-of-boasting boy,
For he'd had enough of sea to understand.
    He went back amongst his fellows
  Just as gentle as a lamb,
Nor was ever known again to leave the shore,
    And though formerly a bellows
  Would have given him the palm,
From that out he never boasted any more.

# BECAUSE OF THE IRISH THAT'S IN ME.

This song was written as a contribution to an amateur newspaper called the *Longfellow's Literary Review*, read at a meeting of a society of the same name held at Juneau on the 17th of March, 1891.

It was composed just before Parnell's death, and while he was laboring under a cloud occasioned by his exposé in the great O'Shea divorce suit.

"The Irish that's in me" is that which I obtained from my mother, both of whose parents, I am proud to say, were originally from the land of Erin and Shamrocks.

What makes me feel angry when Ireland's traduced?
 It's because of the Irish that's in me.
Why drink I so deep to an Irishman's toast?
 It's because of the Irish that's in me.
What makes my blood boil when I think of the laws
(Of hard times in Ireland the positive cause)
Encroaching on freedom, then asking applause?
 It's because of the Irish that's in me.

What makes me resent being wound like a spool?
 It's because of the Irish that's in me.
Why am I so ready to fight for Home Rule?
 It's because of the Irish that's in me.
Why do I like Gladstone, can anyone tell?
Why do I descend to stand up for Parnell?
What makes me remember that angels once fell?
 It's because of the Irish that's in me.

Oh, why am I soothed when "Killarney" is sung?
 It's because of the Irish that's in me.
And why does Moore's "Tara" to memory cling?
 It's because of the Irish that's in me.
Why have I a right to aspire to the fame
Of a Goldsmith's, a Steele's, a Sheridan's name?
For leanings to Gulliver, what is to blame?
 It's because of the Irish that's in me.

Why is it I relish an Irishman's wit?
    It's because of the Irish that's in me.
What sets me uproarious when Pat makes a hit?
    It's because of the Irish that's in me.
When an Irish girl, roguish, and buxom, and coy,
Smiles sweetly and calls me the broth of a boy;
Why is it I almost flow over with joy?
    It's because of the Irish that's in me.

Why is it I always am making mistakes?
    It's because of the Irish that's in me.
Why is it I'm prone to say "jabbers and faix"?
    It's because of the Irish that's in me.
When sev'nteenth of Ireland 'round on us has worn,
Explain why with Shamrocks my coat I adorn,
Singing gaily " St. Patrick's Day in the Morn"?
    It's because of the Irish that's in me.

Why is it I'm careless in fixing my duds?
    It's because of the Irish that's in me.
Why am I enamor'd of Murphies and spuds?
    It's because of the Irish that's in me.
When the "cratur's" around, what makes me so shy?
And why do I watch it with wistfullest eye?
Then find in surprise I'm infernally dry?
    It's because of the Irish that's in me.

Why am I a post at which everyone kicks?
    It's because of the Irish that's in me.
Why is my poor head a fam'd target for bricks?
    It's because of the Irish that's in me.
Why do I forgive and forget ev'ry frown?
And sing to amuse and make friends like a clown?
When ev'ryone's wishing for me to sit down?
    It's because of the Irish that's in me.

(As an encore)

What makes you all wild now to hear an encore ?
    It's because of the Irish that's in me.
Why on my weak efforts such plaudits you pour ?
    It's because of the Irish that's in me.
But, friends, I've too often the Blarney stone kissed ;
Protection I'll find behind Sullivan's fist ;
Defending my honor, your necks he will twist ;
    All because of the Irish that's in me.

---

## A SONG OF THE WALTZ.

The world may be full of grim sorrow and care,
    Of tri'ls, tribulations and woe ;
And tyranny, poverty, want and despair
    May meet us wherever we go ;
But if we would fly for a moment's respite,
    From its ghouls, and its griefs, and its faults,
Let us banish our care, swinging maidenhood fair
    In the mystical maze of the waltz.
        Hurling, whirling, twisting, twirling,
            Lost in the maze of the waltz ;
        The world may have ailings, and sorrows, and
            failings,
        But not while we're dancing the waltz.

They say that it's wicked and hurtful to dance,—
    A case of sour grapes, to be sure ;
Thank heaven that one has so often the chance
    To practise a pleasure so pure :
When the music melts into melody sweet,
    And mingles its marches and halts,
One indeed is amiss, who can feel aught but bliss,
    While whirling around in the waltz ?

Hurling, whirling, twisting, twirling,
    Lost in the maze of the waltz ;
The world may have ailings, and sorrows, and
    failings,
    But not while we're dancing the waltz.

We feel as we glide o'er the well polished floor
    We are sailing on fairy seas ;
That our feet take the place of the rythmic oar,
    And music's our zephyr-like breeze ;
Then away we go in oblivious glee,
    Quite free from all worldly assaults,
And the fairies all sing of the flowers of Spring
    To gladden our hearts as we waltz.

Hurling, whirling, twisting, twirling,
    Lost in the maze of the waltz ;
The world may have ailings, and sorrows, and
    failings,
    But not while we're dancing the waltz.

---

## MOORE, BYRON AND SCOTT.

When an Irishman's dull, enervated and sad ;
    When his heart calls for sympathy dear ;
When far from his country he wanders abroad
    On a soil that is foreign and drear ;
Whose strains can recall to his memory, home,
    And induce him his lot to endure,
And do honor to Ireland where'er he may roam,
    Like the soul-stirring lyrics of Moore ?

When an Englishman, proud of the land of his birth,
    So conceitedly to it refers,
And receives a reproach for the marvelous dearth
    Of the singers whom true passion stirs.
Just notice the light that comes into his eye,
    And illumines his features of iron,
As he says with accents that reason defy :—
    " You've forgotten our passionate Byron."

When a Scotchman—the tasks of his day being done—
    Wants a moment of bliss less alloy ;
And has laid aside Burns, Coila's own darling son,
    For diversion and spice in his joy ;
Whose pages are full of the patriot's song,—
    Of the battles that Scotchmen have fought ?
To whose minstrel raptures does genius belong,
    If not found in those written by Scott ?

To our century's childhood the world owes a debt,
    'Twill take ages and ages to pay ;
For posterity sure will be loth to forget
    The names introduced in my lay.
Three friends and three poets, all equal in fame—
    Though of different races begot ;
Whose genius all nations now proudly proclaim,
    And thank God for Moore, Byron and Scott.

---

## THE SOON-TO-BE DESERTED VILLAGE.

Alaska, as everybody knows, is a very large territory. In the absence
of a civilized population, this vastness of area has some disadvantageous
sides to it. In no way, however, is it so annoying as at the semi-annual
sittings of the district court, when, in order to get a grand jury together,
subpœnas have to be sent out over a distance of several hundred miles.
The court is usually held at Sitka, the capital, although by far the greater
number of jurors have to be summoned from Juneau, the largest town—
unfortunately, some 200 miles away. The Juneauites do not like this three
week compulsory vacation. In fact, old records, doctors' certificates,
etc., etc., are never in such great demand. Those, however, who are
compelled to go, make the best of a bad bargain, and consequently
quiet, dreamy, old Sitka is like a pandemonium while the "boys" are
there. It was on one of these occasions that the poem below first saw the
light. It was published in the Juneau *Mining Record* a few days before
the "courting" citizens were expected back ; and although the author
would not have faced Goldsmith for the world after imitating him so
badly, it gave him considerable satisfaction, a few hours after its anony-

mous publication, to have an old timer in the country recite the poem almost
from beginning to end before an applauding audience, with the ejaculation :
"Gentlemen, that tells you all you want to know about Sitka."

Sweet Sitka, loveliest village of the wild,
Undimmed attraction to the wandering child;
Where Fall and Winter 'merged in one do stay
Till tardy Spring their torrents drives away ;
And where, when Summer comes, thy lonely charms to kiss,
No other clime can boast such short-lived reign of bliss.
How often have I climbed thy castle's height serene ;—
And gazed abroad amazed, upon the varied scene,
Close bounded by the tombs upon a neighb'ring steep,
Where rude forefathers of the savage Siwash sleep.
How oft in pensive mood through native ranch I've strolled,
Or by the barracks grim and Russian buildings old ;
Beside the great Greek church, the tumble-down fire hall ;
The aged, worn-out mill, and mission buildings all ;
Or paced that only road, to lovers doubly dear,
That leads to nature's haunts and Indian river near.
But Sitka, like sweet Auburn, of whose fate we all have read,
Is dying, slowly dying ;—after court she will be dead.

## CHRISTMAS, 1890.

There are no railroads or telegraph lines in Alaska yet. The arrival
of the bi-monthly steamer with mail and provisions from "below" (as
anywhere south of that country is called) is consequently an event of no-
small moment. At Juneau, Sitka, Wrangel, or, in fact, any of the settle-
ments at which it calls, the approach of the steamer at any hour of the day
or night is the signal for a hurry and bustle that would do credit to a
town ten times their combined size. Even the usually stoical natives
are noticed to get a move on. The small boys, and many of the bigger
ones, too, for that matter, set up a series of catcalls, halloos and yells of
"steamboat," which, added to the deep resounding whistle of the vessel as
it gives warning of its arrival, makes it utterly impossible for anyone to
live within a mile of the settlement and not know that the mail boat has
arrived. Juneau is composed entirely of "wanderers from home," so
that some of the feelings portrayed in "Xmas, 1890" are pretty common
property among the prodigals in that far away part of our continent.

Tidings from home ! Glad tidings from home !
Christmas morning, and tidings from home !
Ring out, ye wild bells, till your tongues you destroy ;
You cannot interpret a tithe of my joy.

To-day when I wakened from sleep to my fate,
My heart was weighed down with my lonely estate ;
In sadness I nurtured each grief and each care ;—
And the thought that 'twas Christmas increased my despair :
So when out pierced the cry of "Steamboat ! the steam-
      boat ! "
A slight choking sensation welled up in my throat;
But on pond'ring a moment, thinks I, with a groan,
There'll be nothing for me, I'm forgotten and lone ;
Yet still a faint hope goaded onward my feet
To the post-office building—all Juneau's retreat,
But there in a corner, shame-faced I stood,
Till the crowd had dispersed with their tidings of good ;
For I feared to be told with the people around,
That for "Currie, Geo. G." not a note could be found.
When the office was clear, to the wicket I went,
And with nonchalant air gave anxiety vent ;
And then with a quick beating heart in my breast,
Waited doubtfully hopeful to see was I blest :
Imagine my wonder, excuse my surprise,
As incredulous gazing I saw 'fore my eyes,
Not one, but six letters in handwriting dear,
Addressed to myself quite convincingly clear ;
I grabbed them elate,—broke open each seal ;
And devoured their contents with a feverish zeal ;
And my rapture grew greater as I in my glee
Read the heaps of kind wishes there written for me;
For among the loved names that appeared at the ends,
Were those of my father, my sister, and friends.

Tidings from home ! Glad tidings from home !
Christmas morning, with tidings from home !
Ring out, ye wild bells, till your tongues you destroy ;
You cannot interpret a tithe of my joy.

## THE SEASONS.

When wintry winds around us blow
   Their chill and icy blast ;
When earth is buried deep in snow,
   And autumn's charms are past ;
'Tis then the joys, that most we prize,
   Like summer birds take wing ;
'Tis then, with vaguely longing hearts,
   We sigh for smiling spring.

Spring comes ! an 1 ev'ry glowing breast,
   Responsive to its power,
With health and hope, twice doubly blest,
   New blossoms with the flower.
The earth, aroused from wintry lair,
   Bedecks itself in green,
And, glad to find its form so fair,
   Smiles forth—a perfect scene.

But that bright orb, in whom sweet May
   Put all her early trust,
Now stronger grown, with heated ray
   Has laid her 'neath his dust.
While hill and dale, no longer gre en,
   But yellow—stubbled—dry,
Can ill repress their envy keen
   Of summer's placid sky.

At last, among the tinted trees,
   With wild and wailing sound,

The wind once more strips branches bare,
    And strews their leaves around ;
The day again grows short and cool,
    And night—its chosen bier—
Approaches close with misty shroud,
    To clasp the dying year.

## INTOLERATION.

What makes men contemn the poor negro's black face,
    And hold Indians in detestation ;
What makes them think Mongols quite foreign to grace ?
    It's racial intoleration.

What first causes strife—then develops to war,
    What scatters abroad desolation ;
What robs our exchequers of treasure in store ?
    It's national intoleration.

Why do men of party so arrogant grow,
    When theirs is the administration ;
What makes them despise their opponents, and blow ?
    Political intoleration.

Why are we divided in classes and caste,
    According to wealth, birth or station ;
And why do the higher, inferiors detest ?
    Positional intoleration.

Why do temp'rance advocates cause so much harm,
    Instead of their kind's elevation ;
What steals from their efforts the pleasure and charm ?
    Fanatical intoleration.

Why are there so many agnostics abroad,
    Who fain would profess adoration ;
But scarcely know how—so beclouded is God ?
    It's bigoted intoleration.

Ah friends, 'tis a shameful, a lasting disgrace,
    A slur on our civilization,
To think that in life's short and uncertain race
    We find time for intoleration.

If " do unto others as others should do
    Unto us " were our inspiration,
How quickly we would all intolerance rue,
    And practise and preach toleration.

Come then, let us listen with receptive ear
    To ev'ry creed, color and nation ;
Nor thrust one aside as too lowly to hear,
    For that would be intoleration.

## LINES.

(Composed in the heat of a few sincere moments on Sunday, Dec. 2nd,
  1888.)

To Thee, oh God! in my despair
I pen this earnest heart-made prayer

In hopes that Thou, who art divine,
Wilt cleanse my soul and make it thine.

I know I am not worth Thy thought,
My very frame with sin is fraught :

But still because Thy work I am,
For self-made wounds provide a balm.

Give me a salve that sure will heal
My broken spirit and my will.

To Passion, God, I am a slave ;
A shie d from it I fairly crave.

Thou know'st my weakness and canst see
The cure Thou shouldst prescribe for me.

To curb myself in vain I've tried,—
My loathed desire can't be denied.

So now to Thee I humbly kneel,
And pen the words Thou know'st I feel.

In pity, God, look down, and be
A comforter and strength to me.

Help me once more to raise my head
In triumph o'er my passions dead.

And then, oh God, through all my days,
My very life shall sing thy praise.

---

## BACHELOR'S HALL.

Greatest poets have sung with a rapturous swell,
　Of their country, their home, or their friends ;
They've detailed to their readers each ecstatic spell
　That on some dark-eyed maiden depends.
But there's one thing on which they have silently gazed,
　And have mentioned it never at all ;
And a theme without doubt they ought most to have praised
　Is " The pleasures of Bachelor's Hall."

　(*Chorus*)

　　　Oh, the pleasures of Bachelor's Hall ;
　　　Oh, the pleasures of Bachelor's Hall ;
　　A theme without doubt that ought most to be praised
　　　Is the pleasures of Bachelor's Hall.

You have no boardin' missis to measure your feeds ;
　To transform your old boots into steak ;
And when pay-day comes round with its much pressing needs
　The big half of your wages to take.

You've no one to hint that it's getting quite late,
   When a friend comes to give you a call ;
And when out after ten you've no reasons to state,
   In the pleasures of Bachelor's Hall.

You've no parents or loved ones to chide you for nought,
   No brother to give you a " breeze,"
No sisters, or cousins, or aunts to be fought,
   When trying to plague or to tease.
You've no wife to object to your being to club,
   No children around you to squall ;
No dressmaker's bills ! ah there is the rub—
   In the pleasures of Bachelor's Hall.

You go out when you like and come in when you choose,
   There is no one to order you 'round ;
If you place a thing by and lie down for a snooze,
   When you wake you know where it is found.
When you're hungry you've only to stifle the pang
   From your cupboard well stocked near the wall ;
And such comforts, my friends, quite exclusive belong
   To the pleasures of Bachelor's Hall.

---

## AU REVOIR TO 1890.

I sat by the fireside, sobbing, sighing,
To think that the year was slowly dying,
When to stop its course was useless trying,
      All power was vain.

Old '90 had lived its allotted space,
It had run Life's short and fitful race,
And would soon join in *en route* to grace
      The gospel train.

And as I sat,—saw the embers glowing,
Thinks I, while the wind outside was blowing,
Had '90 for me a healthy showing,
              Or otherwise ?

And I pondered it o'er with weighty thought,
Recalled each trifling bliss it brought,
But alas ! found no great good it wrought,
              That I might prize.

The whole year almost from beginning,
Despite resolves, had found me sinning ;
And this kept in my mem'ry dinning,
              As there I mused.

Why should I then its death regret ?
Ah ! there's the rub, that makes me fret :
I'd fain the reason quite forget,
              Till more enthused.

You see—or rather—. now I'm vexed ;
Such prying questions make me mixed ;
You should not, Thought, get persons fixed
              In such a box.

I liked old '90 spite of trouble,
E'en though my sins increased to double,
Though life seemed scarcely worth a bubble,
              To most of folks.

So now, old pard, God speed you well,
And keep you free of far famed h—l ;
Some wished you there this long long spell,—
              The rascal crew.

And since young '91 you're here,
I'll stand the treats : cigars or beer ?
You're hardly old enough, I fear,
              For stronger stew.

But hold !   The temp'rance men might shout,
And call me villain out and out ;
For tempting you their worth to doubt ;
        Alack the day !

" So gie's your hand, we'll aye be friends "
(As Sandy says) to make amends ;
And that your stay no ill forfends,
        We'll trust and pray.

In Juneau, that's where I'm residing,
The boys need someone by for chiding ;
I hope you'll do some trusty guiding,
        And guard them true.

And when, my friend, your hours are ending,
When life with death is slowly blending,
I think—I know without contending,
        I'll sigh for you.

---

## THE SONG OF A WOOD-PILE.

I wintered one season at—you know,
  Where the weather is awfully chill ;
And the wind it blew fierce through the windows,
  With a fury that boded me ill ;
I had to my name scarce a dollar,—
  I lived à la poverty style ;
And the one friend I had in my squalor
  Was a rousing, substantial wood-pile.
      But I sighed as I looked on that wood-pile,
        As I gazed on it day after day ;
      Yes, I sighed as I looked on that wood-pile,
        And saw that it dwindled away.

When the winter first came with its blizzards,
  Says I to myself with a smile :

"If all of my other friends fail me
  I'll still have that rousing wood-pile."
I strutted about in my gladness,
  And naught could diminish my glee;
Thinks I, "Who could languish in sadness,
  And have such a wood-pile to see?"
      But I sighed as I looked on that wood-pile,
        As I gazed on it day after day;
      Yes, I sighed as I looked on that wood-pile,
        And saw that it dwindled away.

It seemed cold as icebergs for ages;
  The winter was long and severe;
So I kept piling wood in my heater,
  Regardless that woodpiles were dear.
The weather was just at its coldest,
  When lo! I was horribly pained
To find, though I'm one of the boldest,
  No stick of my wood-pile remained.
      So I sighed as I looked for that wood-pile,
        I sighed as I gazed in dismay;
      So I sighed as I looked for that wood-pile,
        When the wood-pile had dwindled away.

And now, friends, I'll tell you the moral,—
  The moral of this little lay;
And you'll hear what is taught by a wood-pile,—
  A wood-pile that dwindles away;
When the winter ne'er seems to be going,
  But the wood goes in spite of your sigh;
While the snow and the wind keep a-blowing,—
  Get another big wood-pile or—die.
      For to sigh as you gaze on a wood-pile,
        To sigh as you gaze in dismay;
      For to sigh as you gaze on a wood-pile
        Don't keep it from dwindling away.

## THE GOOD OLD TIMES

While on my couch at even's close,
  My work and worry o'er,
I lay me down in brief repose,
  To think of bliss in store ;
My mem'ry flits to other climes,
  And musingly I sigh,
To live again those good old times—
  Those good old times gone by.

The pleasures that are mine to-day
  May seem without alloy ;
New friends may be as blithe and gay ;
  New hopes as full of joy ;
But spite of present merry chimes,
  My thoughts still backward fly,
To revel with those good old times—
  Those good old times gone by.

My days were brighter then than now ;
  Ambition seem'd more real ;
Ill luck I faced with dauntless brow,
  And scorned, where now I kneel.
But why bewail my lot in rhymes,
  And o'er spilt water cry ?
They've been and gone, those good old times—
  Those good old times gone by.

And as the years quite tirelessly
  Speed onward while I creep,
I've ev'ry reason to believe
  They'll steal my fitful sleep;
But I'll forgive such petty crimes,
  If, as I wakeful lie,
I can recall those good old times—
  Those good old times gone by.

## IT IS MY COUNTRY!

Canada, Canada, home of the free !
Thousands of heroes do homage to thee :

Homage thou well hast deserved at their hand,
For happy are they who dwell in thy land.

Hail to thy meadows so fertile and vast ;
Hail to thy woodlands, by none they're surpassed ;

Hail to thy mountains, so stately and high ;
Hail to thy rivers, miraged in the sky ;

Hail to thy sons, who in battle so brave,
Show but the courage thy liberty gave ;

Hail to thy daughters, so noble and pure,
Filled with thy sweetness so fresh and demure ;

Though Fate leads my footsteps to lands o'er the sea
I'll never be subject to any but thee.

---

## MISERY.

Blow on, ye northern winds, blow on,
   Let nothing cause your rage to stay ;
If mortals totter and look wan,
   What matters it?—they are but clay.

Make fiercer still your icy blast
   In fury though it never end ;
An angry sky with black o'ercast
   To mis'ry not a jot can lend.

Shine on, in mock'ry, Sun, shine on,
   Your blazing heat around us spread ;
From darkest night bring forth the dawn,
   Or raise to life the winter's dead.

Though mighty forests you may burn ;
　　Or cause deep rivers to run dry :
If mortals but in sorrow mourn,
　　Despite thy power they'll weep or—die.

---

## DRIFTING WITH THE TIDE.

Commemorative of the moonlight return in row-boats from several
private picnics to Nun's Island—a large and hospitable piece of property,
dividing the St. Lawrence River some 3 miles below Lachine Rapids.

Come launch the boat together, boys,
　　The night is drawing on ;
Old Time we cannot tether, boys,
　　A pleasant day has gone ;
Pull out across the waters, boys,
　　That from the Rapids glide,
And let the throng, in happy song,
　　Go drifting with the tide.

### CHORUS.

Drifting with the tide, drifting with the tide,
O'er the rippling eddies, right merrily we glide.
Who can paint the pleasures of that happy, happy ride ;
As formed in grand flotilla we drift singing down the tide.

The moon in fitful fancy tries,
　　With many a glitt'ring beam,
To hold the ripples as they rise
　　From dancing down the stream ;
Despairing of her task, she sighs
　　For friendly cloud to hide ;
But listlessly we hear her plea,
　　While drifting with the tide.

*(Chorus.)*

Along the shore like sentries stand
  Grim poplars in the haze ;
Or here and there a maple grand
  Invites our passing praise ;
But though they send from off the land
  Their shadows far to chide ;
In vain they preach, for out of reach
  We're drifting with the tide.

(Chorus.)

With happy heart and lusty throat,
  We sing a common song ;
Since ev'ry well remembered note
  May present bliss prolong.
Too bad we cannot always float,
  Upon Life's current wide ;
And feel the joys of girls and boys,
  While drifting with the tide.

(Chorus.)

## KEEP CLIMBING.

Keep climbing! keep climbing ! no quarter, my boy,
Nor throw early hopes to the wind like a toy ;
Take courage, nor falter ; keep pegging along ;
With higher, up higher, forever your song.

Keep climbing ! keep climbing ! be never cast down,
Though men who seem higher in scornfulness frown ;
Just bob up serenely, nor ever look back,
Their manners but prove them upon the wrong track.

Keep climbing ! keep climbing ! though weary and faint ;
Keep upward and onward without a complaint ;
Though friends from the pathway in idleness stray,
Your motto and duty is " Climb while you may."

Keep climbing ! keep climbing ! nor offer to stand,
Or rest in the shadow of what you have planned ;
The way may be rugged, the mountain be steep,
But once on the summit you safely may sleep.

Keep climbing ! keep climbing ! make each movement tell,
A thing that's worth doing is worth doing well;
The goal is above you, defeat is below,
Keep climbing ! keep climbing ! to victory go.

## THE LAND OF THE RISING SUN.

They may talk of the West, of the wild woolly West,
   With its valleys and mountains of gold
Where the bear and the beaver alone can molest
   The miner who delves in its mould ;
Yet in spite of its wonders, its wealth, and its weald,
   E'en though they be ten times increased,
To my sad aching heart, they can never impart
   The joys that were mine in the East.

It was there that I first saw the light of the day,
   And when boyhood upon me had crept,
Where I rambled and gamboled, or, tired out with play,
   On pillows of innocence slept ;
Where in youth, somewhat sobered, in booklore I delved
   To find out its treasures and worth,
Or in social debate with companions sedate,
   On subjects abstruse have held forth.

It was there that young Cupid discovered my heart,
   And despite all my struggles and wiles
Sent with unerring aim his most dangerous dart,—
   For I've been ever since in his toils ;
'Twas there, too, ambition first harrowed my brain,
   And before I was even aware,
Set me chisel in hand, carving futures in sand,
   And building up castles in air.

It is there that my sister, kind-hearted and true,
  Plods peacefully onward through life ;
And 'tis there that my brother bade early adieu
  To earth's pleasure and passion and strife ;
It is there 'neath the sod, all oblivious to care,
  That my father and mother lie low,
While the grass o'er their graves, in the breeze gently waves,
  And beckons wherever I go.

Though to far foreign climes my fleet fate I pursue,
  Still my thoughts ever backward do roam,
And I often recall my last ling'ring adieu
  To the friends in that dear distant home ;
And I sigh for a time which will certainly come,
  When my longings and wand'rings have ceased ;
Then its thither I'll fly, there to settle and die,
  Near my dear native home in the East.

## JUBILEE ODE.

[Written in Montreal, Canada, on June 21, 1887.]

Blow loud and long the trumpets,
  Let music fill the air ;
Rejoice, rejoice, ye patriots ;
  Shake off all toilsome care.
Come forth, ye faithful subjects,
  And shout the glad'ning strain ;
Sing out the glorious gospel—
  Victoria still doth reign.

Through fifty long and changing years,
  With firm yet loving hand,
She's carried out a nation's will,
  And boldly ta'en her stand ;
Her sway is felt o'er land and wave,
  And many a distant shore
This day resounds with notes of praise
  For her whom we adore.

Then let us all in unison
　　Sing out the joyful tune ;
Our queen in truth wears golden crown,
　　This twenty-first of June.
Come all ye loyal maidens,
　　Chant our triumphal glee ;
With one accord we'll celebrate
　　Onr Sov'reign's Jubilee.

# EARLY POEMS.

# MOTHER.

Dearest mother, whither art thou?
  Why have I been left alone?
Why by thee was I forsaken,
  Ere thy worth was barely known?

Mother—darling, angel mother!
  Can I never see you more?
Have you gone from us forever,
  To that dark eternal shore?

Will you not at my entreaty
  Once again to earth return?
Why, oh why, I pray thee, mother,
  Am I left thy loss to mourn?

How I've longed to have your guidance,
  None but God above can tell;
Just one look of kindness from thee,
  Just to know you wish me well.

When with grief and sorrow stricken,
  Then oh how I yearn for thee!
That I might confide my troubles
  And receive your sympathy.

And to think I don't remember
  Even how you used to smile,
Or how you with love maternal
  Did my baby hours beguile.

Mother—dearest, darling mother!
  How thy name alone can thrill!
Oh, that some divine inspirer,
  Could unfold to me thy will.

E

If there is a place called heaven,—
　Free from trouble, strife and fear,—
Then it's there I hope to meet thee,
　Darling, angel, mother dear.

---

## AN IDEAL PICNIC.

Across the stream, amid the trees
　And fragrant fields of grass,
Each lad of our acquaintance good
　Asked o'er some charming lass.

A fire of brushwood soon was built,
　O'er which a pot was hung ;
And what we found too raw to eat
　Within that pot was flung.

The water soon began to boil,
　And then we had some tea ;
And those who don't believe we ate
　Should have been there to see.

We cleaned the baskets one by one,
　Of their delicious load,
Of fish and meat and cakes and pie
　And berries *à la mode*.

But luncheon o'er we quick began
　To skip and play quite curious,
In fact, to quote from Bobby Burns,
　The fun grew fast and furious.

A lovely time indeed was spent
　With hammocks, swings and such ;
While parlor quoits and croquet, too,
　Took up attention much.

'Twas midnight past before we thought
    Of ending up the day,
And then with ev'ry basket light
    We homeward bent our way.

The only drawback to our sport,
    Amid those fields of grass,
Was this,—a trifling one, 'tis true—
    *It never came to pass.*

---

## THE ROSCOE CLUB.

When I was about 19 years of age, three of my most intimate friends formed with me the nucleus of a literary society. Chancing on our second or third evening to become interested in Washington Irving's sketch book, our attention was fixed on his delightful little notice of Wm. Roscoe, Liverpool's literary star. The high character and attainments of that gentleman, as eulogized by Irving, seemed almost the personification of the avowed object of our little circle, and we forthwith dubbed ourselves the Roscoe Club in honor of him. Time and the inroads of death have scattered the four original members almost as effectively as though those devastators were created for no other purpose ; but the club still lives, and yet cherishes the hope of seeing the prophecy contained in the last stanza of the following verses proved beyond peradventure.

On each happy Tuesday night,
    When the moon is shining bright,
And the stars within the firmament do glow ;
    We convene the favored four,
    And with literary lore,
We beguile the hours away in Club Roscoe.

Though the rain in torrents falls,
    And the lightning's flash appals ;
Though old Boreas a hurricane doth blow ;
    Still we gather 'round the board,
    On which choicest books are stored,
And we spend the evening in our Club Roscoe.

When the leaves all turning red,
    And the ripened fruit o'erhead,
Both proclaim that Autumn's bliss we soon shall know ;
    Though our friends stroll up the road,—
    Arm in arm quite *à la mode*—
We're content to pass our time in Club Roscoe.

When the nights grow cold and long,
    And the winds blow fierce and strong,
And the ground is hard and crisp with ice and snow ;
    We draw near the glowing grate,
    And with heart and voice elate,
We discuss the future of our Club Roscoe.

When the Spring in garments green
    Changes fast the wintry scene,
And to ev'ry living thing its gifts bestow ;
    With new life and vigor filled,
    And as critics better skilled,
Are the members of that dear old Club Roscoe.

Though its roll contains but few,
    Yet each heart is stout and true,
Which in after years the world will surely know ;
    And if time works all things well,
    As a prophet I foretell,—
Famous far will be our little Club Roscoe.

———

## A PRAYER.

Thy greatness, God, I cannot know,
    I cannot guess Thy powers;
But ev'ry earnest thought must show
How I revere Thy works below
    Upon this world of ours.

And still I do not know they're Thine,
   I only think 'tis so;
I know not where to draw the line,
But hope in sooth they are a sign
   Of what from Thee can grow.

If all omnipotent Thou art,
   As something seems to say;
Oh, put the truth into my heart,
And let me *know* I am a part
   Worth more to Thee than clay.

Oh teach me that thou hast a care
   For ev'rything I do;
And answer this my earnest prayer,
Lest I be plunged in dark despair,
   With nought to help me through.

And if, oh God, Thou art supreme,
   And rulest all that's here;
May I be taught to do, not dream,
Pray make me ever what I seem,
   And keep my soul sincere.
                  Amen.

---

## WHEN WE'RE DEAD AND GONE.

Wondrous things may come to pass,
   When we're dead and gone;
Nothing ancient can surpass,
   When we're dead and gone;
Stars in heaven may collide,
And the sun with rapid stride
May o'ertake the moon, his bride,
   When we're dead and gone.

Gravitation's law may burst,
   When we're dead and gone,
Which of mishaps is the worst,
   When we're dead and gone ;
Mortals from this world would fall,
Into night and chaos sprawl,
Where grim darkness would appal,
   When we're dead and gone.

Earth its bowels may unfold,
   When we're dead and gone,
And yield treasures yet untold,
   When we're dead and gone ;
With eruptions mounts may quake,
Rivers o'er their banks may break.
Oceans may their beds forsake,
   When we're dead and gone.

Men through earth may make a breach,
   When we're dead and gone,
The Antipodes to reach,
   When we're dead and gone :
They in railway cars may roll
Underground from pole to pole,
Paying but a trifling toll,
   When we're dead and gone.

Th'electric source for having found,
   When we're dead and gone,
Inventors great may be renowned,
   When we're dead and gone ;
And through its improvèd ray,
Night may chase its shades away,
And they'll live in endless day,
   When we're dead and gone.

People in machines may fly,
    When we're dead and gone ;
Scaling heights of azure sky,
    When we're dead and gone.
O'er the clouds they'll ride supreme,
And what now does monstrous seem,
May have faded to a dream,
    When we're dead and gone.

P'rhaps we may not need our wings,
    When we're dead and gone ;
Or such like ethereal things,
    When we're dead and gone.
Golden stairs to heaven may rise,
Not in song as you'd surmise,
But which angels won't despise,
    When we're dead and gone.

---

## MARY, THE SCOTTISH FISH-WIFE AND HER DOG.

One afternoon, away back in the eighties, a Scotchman came into the office in which I was employed, and the conversation drifting to Edinburgh, he told about the fish-wives for which that city is noted almost as much as for its castle.   To exemplify his story, the gentleman drew a picture of an orthodox wife with her creel hanging over her back. The sketch being laid to one side, someone else came in shortly after, and in a freak of fancy drew a dog on the same piece of paper.   Both drawings struck me as being worthy of " special mention," and in order to give it such, the company for which I was employed made very little out of me for the remainder of that day.   The following parody was what the picture suggested to my boyish mind :

Mary had a little dog,
    With teeth just like a shark ;
And ev'rything that Mary said,
    Would make that doggie bark.

## HOW I ONCE FELT.

It followed her to town each day,
　Though not against her wish,
For it appears her aim in life
　Was selling caller fish.

And when she sang her humble cry
　Upon the stone-paved street,
The dog to help was never shy,
　But loud her voice did greet.

And as she marches on her way,
　The dog ne'er far behind,
With shaking tail and panting breath,
　Much custom helps to find.

For when the people hear that bark,
　They know that May is nigh ;
And haste to get their dishes out,
　That they some fish may buy.

But should some evil disposed one
　His mistress try to rob,
That dog is there with sharkish teeth,
　To make the culprit sob.

And as this world goes on apace,
　And grows and fades the heather,
These simple two are never seen
　Except they are together.

And as they travelled on through life,
　Their friends found out at length
Their well proved motto had been this :—
　*In unity is strength.*

## TIMELY ADVICE.

O innocent youth, let me warn you to shun
  The life of a book-keeping scribe;
If to you it appears to be easy as fun,
Such a view is quite false, for I've chanced to be one
  Of the long almost heart-broken tribe.

You're supposed to appear at your desk ev'ry day
  As the bell in the steeple strikes eight;
And if after that but a moment you stay,
Alas! what a reck'ning you're destined to pay,
  For the horrible crime—being late.

You never get credit for half that you do,
  You are a continual drudge;
If you venture to say that your work is too-too,
Your superior says in a hillabaloo,
  " You are not the person to judge."

When business is rushing, and work is increased,
  You are asked if you'll stop until ten;
If you dare to refuse, or demur in the least,
The dire threat is soon made that you'll sure be released,
  If you make such a hubbub again.

If you happen to think you are worth an advance;
  In wonder they'll open their eyes;
And the answer, though curt, will be sharp as a lance,
For they'll say they've just been awaiting a chance
  To give you an Irishman's rise.

And more could I tell if I had but the space,
  Of the horrors of this kind of work;
And though it is really no frightful disgrace
To be spending your time in some dingy old place:
  *Take advice, friend, and don't be a clerk.*

## BOSKY DELL.

While bending o'er my daily toil,
   Oppressed by city heat;
And breathing in the dusty soil
   Arising from the street;
Though bearing with resignèd fate
   The noise of city life;
In truth, at t'mes, I'd fain va ate
   Its bustle and its strife.

Before my eyes bright visions pass
   Of fields and meadows green,
Of yellow corn and waving grass,
   And humble rustic scene;
Till thoughts of brooks and shady nooks
   Soon o'er me cast a spell,
And I recall the beauties all,
   Of dear old Bosky Dell.

There stands the cottage small and trim,
   Beside a lordly pine,
That stretches o'er the roof a limb—
   Protection's surest sign.
Its walls are decked with ivy green;
   And roses sweet to smell,
Within the dark rich foliage
   Luxuriantly dwell.

A purling brook some yards away,
   O'er rocks glides rippling on;
And sings its sad incessant lay
   From break of dawn to dawn.
No jarring noise the silence cleaves;
   All sounds are hushed and still;
The sighing wind, the rustling leaves,
   The music of the rill,

Save that at times from many a bower,
　High up each neighb'ring tree,
The birds such floods of music shower,
　The grove is drenched with glee.
Or when from distant meadow land,
　Some petted lamblet's bleat
Is heard as 'round its sober dam
　It skips with tireless feet.


Some sweet breathed kine, neath friendly shade,
　In lazy languor lie,
With munching mouth, and shaking head,
　And dreamy half-shut eye.
But as this scene before me lies
　In panoramic view,
Faint twinkling vapors slow arise,
　And twilight does ensue.


Then O ! to see the grandeur now
　That spreads itself around :
The moon from yonder mountain brow
　With silver tints the ground ;
The stars within her train appear,
　And soon the vault of night
Is sprinkled o'er with jewels clear
　And diamonds sparkling bright.


A still and awful silence takes
　Possession of the air ;
Till trees, and fields, and birds seem all
　In Nature's solemn care.
O ! fain I would some more relate
　Upon this pleasing theme,
But here I woke, and to my fate,
　Found Bosky Dell a dream.

## A COMPOSITION.

Roscoe Club, the origin and objects of which have already been mentioned in these pages, on one occasion demanded essays from its members upon the various phases of government in vogue during the present age.   The Czar or absolute monarchy was the particular kind that fell to the author's lot. In the absence of any statistical knowledge upon the subject, this " Composition," which is self-explanatory, was utilized to fill up the gap.

Dear friends, 'twas my duty to write out to-night,
An essay of length on the Czar and his might ;
And had I had power to do what I ought,
An essay no doubt I to you would have brought ;
But the subject you see had so much in its train,
All my efforts to grasp it I found were in vain ;
So you'll please be content if what little I tell,
You have known long ago perhaps perfectly well ;
And as custom has classed all chestnuts with crime,
To make it seem new I will tell it in rhyme.

The Czar, we are told in the books used at school,
Is a monarch who governs with absolute rule ;
Not like our good queen at the beck and the call
Of a Gladstone, a Churchill, a Bright or a Sal.;
But a king at whose bidding men die at the stake,
One word from whose lips can make all Europe quake.
He has but to look, and faint hearts cease to beat ;
He wills, and all Russia must cringe at his feet ;
For justice his subjects appeal to the throne,
It rests on his word and his judgment alone.

But despite all his pow'r, deny it who can,
This tyrant of millions is only a man ;
And as such you doubtless have seen in the papers,
How much he's harassed by those nihilist capers ;
And though Fortune's child, he is in constant dread,

Lest an hour deprive him of sceptre and head.
With this, my dear friends, I'm afraid I must end, —
No more to my verse has my knowledge to lend ;
But perhaps if ever I travel to Moscow,
I'll visit the Czar for the good of the Roscoe.

---

## ODE TO A SKULL.

Every poet has patrons. The first person to patronize and encourage my boyish efforts in the art of rhyming was Mr. J. B. Forbes, at that time of Montreal, but now a resident of Pt. Levi, Que. This gentleman is a passionate admirer of poetry, and can quote passages from Burns, Byron or Shakespeare by the hour. Seeing some of my earliest effusions by chance one day, instead of holding them and me up to the ridicule that I shamefacedly expected, he immediately took an interest in my scribblings praised them up sky high, and as a test of my powers proposed that I imagine myself in a grave-yard with a skull that I had picked up from curiosity in my hand. The train of thought to which such an incident happened to give rise he desired me to put in rhyme, and, being my employer, as an incentive he kindly allowed me what spare time he could afford during the remainder of the day for that purpose. Grateful for his well meant flattery, and anxious to keep up my new reputation, by night-fall I managed to have this concoction ready for his amused perusal. It has several very palpable faults, but I feel proud of it nevertheless, as a production of my 16th year.

Alas ! Alas ! how sad I feel
   When on this skull I gaze ;
For 'neath its shell a something real
   Did dwell in brighter days,
And thought or dreamed of future life
   Upon this world of sorrow,
And battled with its sins and strife,
   In hopes of peace to-morrow.

Perhaps ambition filled each vein
  Which through this brain did flow,
And helped great schemes of future gain
  To start, and then to grow;
Maybe the wisest plans e'er made
  Took root within this head,
And would have been before us laid,
  Had death not come instead.

Perhaps this may have been the skull
  Of someone of renown,
Whose works of genius now are known
  To Earth's remotest town ;
Or p'raps some conscience-stricken wretch
  Could have no solace here,
And so mid suicidal itch
  Did end his life in fear.

Perhaps, again, this once has been
  The head of some great wit,
Whose faculties were ever keen
  To make some happy hit.
Or was some idiotic mind
  Once hid beneath this shell,
That to good sense was ever blind,
  Whatever else befell ?

Perhaps some farmer might this claim,
  If he were now on earth,
Whose easy-going, honest aim
  If known might prove of worth ;
Or, may be, it did once belong
  To some unlucky devil,
Who barely knew 'twixt right and wrong,
  But died mid maddest revel.

Perhaps some sailor brave and bold,
  With jolly looks, and gay,
Might once beneath this head have rolled
  Across the watery way ;
Or p'raps some soldier fighting hard,
  Away from home and land,
Had this from off his shoulders struck
  By some combatant's hand.

Perhaps it once encovered one
  Who, struggling for his right,
Was killed before his work was done
  By main or money might ;
Perhaps some coward base and mean
  (For all are base who cower)
Might claim this cranium for his own,
  If heav'n would give him power.

Maybe an honest pauper
  Did use this empty head,
In pondering how, and when, and where,
  He'd get a crust of bread.
Or p'raps it once was held erect
  By some vain, haughty man,
Who cared not whom  he crushed direct
  Beneath his selfish ban.

In fact, with truth 'twere hard to guess
  To whom this skull belonged ;
But then for that I care not less,
  Nor would I see it wronged.
The chances are it once did crown
  Some worthy, manly frame,
Who cared not for a world's renown
  While he had his good name.

# LOVE SONGS.

# ZETULBA.

Zetulba, unfortunately, is a purely ideal character. Her name and this poem in its entirety was suggested by the line, " My Zetulba come reign o'er my soul," an alleged quotation from an old French song introduced by Victor Hugo into his great work, *Les Misérables*.

In the soft and quiet twilight,
   When all earth seems wrapped in rest,
And the ruddy trail of daylight
   Fast is fading in the West :

While the stars are twinkling shyly
   From behind their misty shroud,
And the moon is peeping coyly
   Through some silver-edgèd cloud :—

Then for you, my loved Zetulba,
   Throbbings o'er my bosom roll;
And I yearn to have thee, darling,
   Reigning queen within my soul.

Fair Zetulba, sweet Zetulba,
   Dearest guardian of my heart,
Life would seem not worth the living,
   If from thee I had to part.

If thou would'st, my lovely fair one,
   Cheer the life in your control ;
Say that you, oh sweet Zetulba !
   Will reign o'er my troubled soul.

## MY LOVE.

My love is like a lily fair,
　My love is like a rose ;
Her breath with fragrance fills the air,
　Her manner is repose.
My love is very beautiful,
　My love is pure and sweet ;
My love is very dutiful—
　Lacks naught to be complete.

Her eyes, the battlements of love,
　Her weapons of defense,
Guard well that priceless jewel,
　A maiden's innocence ;
Her brow so fair and noble,
　Adorns her queen-like face,
Proclaims her high above the crowd,
　And wisest of her race.

Her cheeks, like morning-glories,
　The glow of youth impart ;
Her dimpled chin and rosy lips
　Would break Apollo's heart ;
Her smile, like sunlit heaven,
　Is radiant and divine,
And speaks of untold happiness
　For he who makes it shine.

Its tinge of heavenly fervor,
　With love and bliss replete,
Enhances her who sends it forth,
　And makes her doubly sweet ;
Her smile—oh thrilling ecstasy !
　Is there for me such joy ?
If so, Zetulba, I'll remain
　Your ever loving boy.

## A TOO ONE-SIDED POET.

Though Burns has praised the banks o' Ayr,
And rhymed with pride of bonnie Doon :
    Could he have dreamed
    What by us streamed,
I fear he would have changed his tune.

Though he has sung of Mauchline belles
And of his sweet Torbolton lasses ;
    Yet 'fore my eye,
    One maiden coy,
Far, all his lovely belles surpasses.

He talks in raptures of his Jean,
And of his darling Highland Mary ;
    But knew he well
    My noble Nell,
His song would doubtless often vary.

## THE DAWN OF HOPE.

These two verses, composed in the summer of 1883, have the particular distinction of being a poet's first tribute at the Shrine of Love.

Oh ! how my breast swells up with joy !
The world can hold no happier boy ;
With pride I dance along the street ;
And my glad heart, how it does beat !
Oh ! how sweet mem'ries bathe my brain !
Love's bliss throughout my soul doth reign ;
Can it be so,—or was I blind ?—
To me fair Ida seemed quite kind.

I think 'tis true, but fearing still,
I wait her awe-inspiring will ;
And oh ! if right my eyes have been ;
No subject could adore his queen
So fondly as I will her grace—
The fairest of God's fairer race ;
And as an acme to my bliss,
I'll beg of her one loving kiss.

---

## A MOMENT OF MUSING.

Once, out in the wilds of Alaska,
  'Neath tents we had raised by the shore
With Steve, a prospector and miner,
  My whilom companion galore ;
While silently nursing a camp-fire
  That crackled as hemlock fires do,
My thoughts, in a moment of musing,
  Took flight, sweet Zetulba, to you.

I saw once again the St. Lawrence—
  The pride of my boyhood and youth—
Whose current majestic flows onward,
  As swift and unfailing as truth.
Victoria bridge, in the distance,
  Lay serpent-like spanning its flood ;
While steamboats beneath the mid archway
  Dragged volumes of smoke as they sped.

On the hillside, the death-mute asylum,
  The dome of St. Peter's so tall ;
The Windsor and other great buildings,
  Recalling to mind Montreal,
Were each, with Mount Royal as background,
  Distinctly portrayed to my view ;
But strange as it sounds, my Zetulba,
  Their forms seemed all blended in you.

Th'occasional bang of the marksman ;'
   The din in the boiler-shop made ;
The noise of the anvil and hammer,
   As workingmen plied at their trade ;
The shriek of the outgoing engine ;
   The rattling of carts on the street ;
Though at one time the bore of existence
   Now fell on my ears like a treat.

I heard, through it all, your sweet laughter,
   And felt for the moment your joy ;
The same thrill of pleasure came o'er me.
   As gladdened my hours while a boy :
I thought, as I gazed on your beauty,
   So real and transparently pure,
How oft it inspired me to duty,
   And deeds that might always endure.

Those hours of the past came to memory,
   When in flights of fancy and love
I traced out a fame-laureled pathway,
   Whereon to win you I must move.
And now, though the hope that allured me
   Has slowly dissolved from the scene,
Like fire that is kindled by matchwood,
   I burn with ambition as keen'

Some day, if I follow my hobby,
   Till the acme of fame has been reached,
I'll credit your siren-like glances
   With the inspiring sermons they've preached ;
And I'll prove to the wayward and doubting
   The worth of the praise I repeat,
By gathering the fame and the laurels
   And throwing them all at your feet.

## GOD KNOWS BEST.

Alone by the ocean in sorrow and sadness,
  I watched the grim breakers come crashing ashore;
Till feeling attuned to their fierce, fitful madness,
  At thoughts of the strife that was mine evermore.
I yearningly gazed on each powerful billow,
  That restlessly rolled o'er the great silent deep,
And wished for the moment to make one my pillow;
  To rock on its writhings in waking and sleep.

Then snapping my fingers in scorn at ambition,
  Away o'er the depths I could speed in my glee;
Now hither and thither with reckless transition—
  The winds nor the waves not more happy or free.
No longer disturbed by desires for to-morrow,
  No longer compelled to submit to defeat ;—
Far off from the causes of shame and of sorrow ;—
  My life would be peacefully, blissfully sweet.

But hold ! if away from the world and its wailing
  My lot all alone on the billows were cast,
Would I not miss some joy for all my plain sailing—
  Some pleasure that all my contentment would blast ?
Ah ! yes ; and I turned from the awful attraction,
  Once more feeling grateful to heaven above :
The pinings, the sorrows, the striving, the faction
  Are nothing if mingled with love,—sweet love.

---

## WESTERN ZEPHYRS.

Oh come to the West, Zetulba,
  To the far away West with me ;
Oh come and be mine, my loved one,
  The star of my hope to be.

The East may have ties that can tether
   To childhood's departing gleam,
But we'll find in the West, together,
   The bliss of a poet's dream.


The sky in that world of wonder
   But seldom is clouded o'er;
No rattle of breaking thunder
   Would startle your slumbers more;
The fields, and the forests, and flowers
   There smile in perennial spring,
While the birds from evergreen bowers
   In song that is ceaseless sing.


By the side of the boundless ocean,
   In a cottage mid roses lost,
We could hallow our heart's devotion,
   Afar from the grovelling host;
The fires of our youthful affection
   Need never grow cold or dim;
For our life, under love's subjection,
   Would glide like a vesper hymn.


Then come to the West, Zetulba,
   To the far away West with me;
Oh come and be mine, my loved one,
   The charm of my life to be.
The East may have ties that can tether
   To childhood's departing gleam,
But we'll find in the West together
   The bliss of a poet's dream.

## A DREAM OF FAIR WOMEN.

One night while on my couch I was reclining,
  While just dozing—lightly dozing on my bed,
I was treated to a vision so refining,
  That for weeks I feared the sight would turn my head.
Before my eyes there passed in slow succession
  All the fair ones who were fam'd in days of yore,
Those goddesses and charmers whose chief mission
  Was to make proud, haughty man the sex adore.

Fair Flora led the van bedecked with flowers,
  Which she strewed on ev'ry side along her way;
While her smiles and rosy blushes fell like showers,
  And refreshed my heated brain like scented spray.
Arm in arm and tripping nimbly o'er the rosebuds,
  Came fair Dian and Euterpe on apace;
While Hygiea followed close upon their footsteps,
  As they started off for pleasure in the chase.

Quite enamor'd of their healthful grace and vigor,
  My senses for the moment seemed benumbed;
Till upon the scene appeared another figure,
  When my heart untouched as yet at last succumbed.
It was Venus, goddess fair of Love and Beauty,
  Who, so perfect, buxom, sonsy, coy and sweet,
Had at length my heart in earnest taken captive,
  And reduced me to a suppliant at her feet.

But alas! the siren goddess left me mourning;
  The procession of enchantment still went on,
And my wounded heart at first within me burning
  Cooled at length until it joyed that she was gone:
For with sober, stately tread came great Minerva,
  The patroness of Science and of Art,
And the smile of recognition that she gave me
  Healed completely my lacerated heart.

Well attended soon came Juno, queen of heaven,
 The fair guardian of married women's bliss ;
Being single, I the shoulder cold was given,
 Which at first I felt inclined to take amiss.
But Erato, who delights to honor lovers,
 And who sympathizes with them in their wrongs,
Happened by most opportunely I imagined
 And sang back my peace of mind with tender songs.

Then methought that fairest Helen, Troy's perdition,
 Followed hard Love's pretty muse upon the scene ;
And at once I understood the fierce condition
 In which Paris, Priam's son, must once have been.
And when Dido made her *début* in the vision,
 I could swear that by the great eternal plan
Not a mortal ever lived, except in fiction,
 Who could spurn such loveliness and yet be man.

Next came Beatrice, whom Dante loved so dearly,
 With Laura—Petrarch's Laura—by her side,
Till quite stricken by their sweetness I sincerely
 Bemoaned with all Italia that they died.
Then Shakespeare's lovely fair ones next paraded,
 And I recognized distinctly as they passed
Soft Ophelia, sweet Portia, good Cordelia,
 Loving Juliet, not the least if mentioned last.

After this my dozing memory seemed to wander,
 Though the ladies loitered still upon the scene ;
But among the last I noticed, I remember,
 Was the shapely form of Burns' bonny Jean.
When, however, my Zetulba stood before me,
 All my frame in liquid bliss she seemed to steep ;
And the vision of fair women flitted from me,
 As in ecstasy I sighed myself to sleep.

# DARLING, I HAVE DREAMED OF THEE.

An answer to the song " Little darling, dream of me."

When with sorrow I'm oppressed,
　And I'm feeling sad and lonely ;
Graham darling, in my breast
　Longings rise for thee, thee only.
Since from me you had to part,
　Dearer hast thou seemed to me ;
Let me whisper to thy heart,—
　Dearest I am dreaming of thee.

　　　Sweetly dreaming, smiling, beaming,
　　　　Brightest visions come to me ;
　　　While the stars were softly gleaming,
　　　　Darling, I have dreamed of thee.

Though deep rivers us divide,
　In my musing hours I hear thee ;
And in slumber by my side,
　Fairies kindly bring thee near me.
Let me now assure thee, love,
　Since thine eyes first beamed on me
Though in distant lands you rove,
　Still I'm ever dreaming of thee.

---

# CUPID'S DIRECTORY.

Who was it took my childish eye,
And liked my boyish hue and cry,—
Who loved me when she knew not why ?
　　　　　　　　'Twas Violet.

Who was it, when both young and small,
I wept because I was not tall,
Smoothed down my ruffled spirits all ?
　　　　　　　　'Twas Emma.

Who was it set my heart on fire,
To think of whom I ne'er could tire,
Whose love did I in vain desire?
                              'Twas Clara.

Who was it as I older grew
My heart into ecstasies threw;
But who at last did prove untrue?
                              'Twas Ida.

Who was it then renewed my bliss,
And could do nought to me amiss,
Then fell out o'er a stolen kiss?
                              'Twas Jessie.

Who after that, with dimpled smile,
And merry wit and maiden wile,
Did ev'ry waking hour beguile?
                              'Twas Celia.

Who was it with her pretty face,
Her lodestone laugh and girlish grace,
Awhile scarce left me breathing space?
                              'Twas Teenie.

Who was it, with her dreamy gaze,
Poetic thoughts and pensive ways,
Helped much to gladden many days?
                              'Twas Amy.

And who ambitions in me raised,
That would before my brain have dazed,
For which her very name be praised?
                              'Twas Nellie.

But who in truth first stole my heart,
And pierced it through with Cupid's dart;
Then caused me many a jealous smart?
                              'Twas Polly.

And who is still my dearest pet,
My lovely laughing-eyed brunette;
Whom think you would I die for yet?
                              'Tis Polly.

----

## PRIMARY IMPRESSIONS.

Written according to agreement, after meeting for the first time a young
lady whose volume of poetry called " Mizpah " I had read some time
before.

'Twas New Year's eve of '88,
   To give that day its dues,
That I with pleasure first did meet
   Fair Helen, Lindsay's Muse.

I had not seen her face before,
   But of her works I'd heard;
And o'er her songs I'd learned to pore,
   Before I saw the bird.

But when we did become acquaint,
   I thought it such a treat,
I sat me down to bardlike paint
   Her qualities complete.

But soon I found 'twas all in vain,
   To tell her traits in verse;
Though fair maids all may wrack my brain
   Fair poets wrack it worse.

I tried each plan my thoughts to bribe;
   But now I must confess,
No words I know with truth describe
   Miss Foote the poetess.

## SHE CAME; WE SAW; SHE CONQUERED.

This piece of blank verse, or poetic prose, or what you will, was composed by request to commemorate Miss K—M—'s visit to Lindsay, Ont., in
the winter of 1888.

'Twas in that cheerless season when from earth's face the
bleak and chilly winds of winter have ruthless chased all hope
of present joy and pleasure ; when Nature, sov'reign dame,
appears her very trust in truth to have deserted ; and when the
frozen ground in shame its coldness hides beneath a veil of
snow—she came.   And at her coming, as if by magic touch,
our hearts, so lonely grown and cold, once more unfolded.
Her gentle influence caused the sunken springs of happiness
to again o'erflow, till soon through ev'ry vein, with energy
renewed, gushes unrestrained the liquid fire of love.   We
saw—and, as we gazed, our tell-tale eyes, replete with mute
astonishment and wonder, plainly showed that such a sight
they ne'er before beheld.   That dark sweet melting face, bedecked with eyes betraying depths of hidden beauty and
crowned with a regal brow o'erhung with locks of waving
loveliness, seems nothing short of perfect.   Her beauteous
countenance. together with those sparkling orbs of pure undimmed intensity, held ev'rybody spellbound, and all must
now confess that in that hour we saw—she queenlike conquered.

---

## THE ST. FRANCIS.

Where St. Francis rippling flows,
　O'er its shallow pebbled bed,
'Twixt fair Melbourne's maple rows,
And the smoke and dust which blows
　Over Richmond's hoary head.

There I met a maiden fair,—
Bright blue eyes and flossy hair,
Full of laughter, full of fun,—
Venus and herself were one ;
  And her name was Edith.

To become her lover bold,
To stroke down those locks of gold,
  With impunity and ease,
Was my constant wish and aim ;
So her maidenship to tame
  I did all I could to please.

  I had nearly won her heart,
  And was overwhelmed with bliss,
In prospect that she soon would be my bride ;
    When my fortunes bade me part
  From this lovely little Miss ;
And all my grief and pain the fates defied.

  Still I think of old St. Francis
  As it ripplingly glides on :
Though away from it I far and farther roam ;
  But the charm that most enhances
  Lies its fertile banks upon,
And is found within a little maiden's home.

———

# EDITH.

There's a maiden whom I love,
  Though she's far away from here ;
Who is known as little Edith kind and true :
  She is like a turtle dove,
  And to me she's very dear,
With her rosy cheeks and laughing eyes of blue.

When we first by chance did meet,
　Little did I think she'd be
In the future such a solace to my heart ;
　But her manner coy and sweet
　Soon has made her dear to me,
And it was a heavy task from her to part.

　When I think of all her charms,
　I flow over with delight ;
But the mem'ry of her distance makes me sad,
　For I'd fain be where my arms
　Could her form encircle tight,
As I whisper loving words to make her glad.

　And what makes me love her more,
　And bemoan my present lot,
In being parted from this little maiden fair,
　Is because in days of yore,
　Which will never be forgot,
She confessed that for me she had a care.

　Should it ever be my bliss,
　In this ever-changing sphere,
To behold again those pretty eyes of blue,
　On her lips I'll plant a kiss,
　And this question will I spear,
" When will you be Edith mine so kind and true? "

## MAGGIE THORP.

Ye Muses list, while I relate
　The sorrows of a lover true ;
And if you've power to mend my fate,
　Still let me not in sorrow sue.
I met the dearest little dame—
　(In vain I tune my wayward harp,
The sweetest music sounds so tame,
　If I but think of Maggie Thorp).

G

I met her, as I said before,
    And straightway Cupid pierced my heart;
And now I gaze—admire—adore,
    But can't withdraw that cruel dart.
Her eyes! Oh ecstasy divine!
    Forgive ye gods, nor with me carp,
When I declare "yours cannot shine,
    As do the eyes of Maggie Thorp."

Her lips! And do I not succumb?
    Why is it that I do not die?
Less blissful thoughts have made me dumb,
    While now I'm able e'en to sigh.
Her lips! Once more let me repeat
    That synonym of heav'nly joy:
That one could find two lips more sweet
    Than Maggie Thorp's I must deny.

And then her hair! By Jove;—but hold,
    To swear but aggravates my woe;
Though reason tells me, " be controlled,"
    I'm reckless 'cause I love her so.
Her witching smile! (Restrain me, Will,
    Lest violence should reign supreme)
Her smile makes less each waking ill,
    And haunts to gladden ev'ry dream.

My plaint is this,—and now, Queen Muse,
    Come close that you my woes may hear,
My loved one smiles and smiles profuse :—
    And lo! 'tis that that makes me drear:
She smiles—but on another swain—
    Which threatens all my plans to warp;
For life can be but grief and pain,
    Unless I wed my Maggie Thorp.

# THE SKUGOG.

This peculiarly named stream is a connecting link in the chain of lakes that almost joins the Georgian Bay with Lake Ontario. The Town of Lindsay is situated upon it, and by too free a use of dams near that place the river, has overflown its banks in many places. The trees with which these banks were at one time covered have died off, leaving nothing now but innumerable stumps to tell of their departed glory.

Though I cannot be ecstatic in my praises,
    Of thy sullen, murky waters stealing on ;
Yet, oh Skugog ! I can sing about the daisies
    That are nurtured, watched and reared thy shores upon.
Though the stumps that stem thy tide when it is swollen
    Are unpicturesque, unlovely, humid, dank ;
Many beauties—Nature's beauties—have been lavished
    With a generous profusion on thy bank.

To enumerate them all would take a life-time,
    While to pass some by unnoticed seems unkind,
So to strike the happy mean and make the verse rhyme
    I will merely name what beauties come to mind.
There is Martha, charming Martha, like a rosebud,
    Shedding beauty, perfume, pleasure all around ;
Making life for those with whom she comes in contact
    With continual surprises to redound.

There is Laura, dark-eyed Laura, tall and slender,
    The desired of all desirings that is known ;
Full of passion, strongest passion, yet so tender,
    For her rashness her good traits do quite atone.
While Jeanie, with her regal gait and carriage,
    Her nobleness of character and mien,
Her pure and honest face nought could disparage,
    Shines o'er her sex a veritable queen.

Then there's laughing Bert, the essence of good nature,
  The picture of enjoyment and of fun ;
With contentment true engraved on ev'ry feature—
  Grand and only the inimitable one.
While her bosom friend and confidant, fair Nellie,
  An open-hearted, frank and loving girl,
With her silv'ry peals of merry tonèd laughter,
  Is to qualify correct a very pearl.

And there's Bessie—simple-hearted little Bessie,
  Full of pity, of endearing ways and wiles ;
True as steel and like a sun-show'r I confess me,
  When through tears burst forth her winsome, happy smiles.
Or there's Aggie, quite as witty as she's gushing,
  In company the acme of desire,
Where she cannot help but be so entertaining,
  That even an Apollo she'd inspire.

And then again—but there, that's quite sufficient
  To set my wond'ring readers all agog ;
And though my weak pen-painting is deficient,
  They'll wish themselves beside the old Skugog.
If I cannot be ecstatic in my praises
  Of thy sullen, murky waters stealing on ;
Yet, oh Skugog ! I can sing about the daisies
  That are nurtured, watched and reared thy shores upon.

## THE CHARM OF HAMILTON.

  I've lived in the Ambitious City,
    Have trodden its streets o'er and o'er ;
  Have sat, to embellish my ditty,
    In beautiful Dundurn and Gore :
  But now that I'm far from the comforts
    And beauties of Hamilton fair ;
  Sweet Allie recalls to my mem'ry
    The scenes that I fain would be near.

I've lain on the side of the mountain,
  O'erlooking this promising town ;
Have drunken, as though from a fountain,
  The entrancing scen'ry aroun' :
But rows upon rows of fine buildings,
  With church spires a-tow'ring to sky,
Seem nought but a network of gildings,
  With Allie's sweet smile in my eye.

In the moonlight I've sailed 'neath the railway,
  Away up Desjardins canal ;
Have rowed through the weird, ghostlike stillness,
  When crickets' faint chirpings appal ;
And yet, though that ride made me tremble,
  While passing the graveyard so drear ;
Still life does its ghouls much resemble,
  When Allie's not by me to cheer.

I have rowed o'er Macassa's still waters,
  To the far-famous Burlington Beach ;
Holding Ontario's waves in its fetters,
  And stowing them out of his reach :
Yet this to a heart-sickened lover
  Seems hardly worth mention at all ;
For I still must continue a rover,
  Till Allie my steps may recall.

---

## BUT SHE IS MY COUSIN.

Refreshing and pure as the glistening dew-drop
  That rests on the lily's pale bosom at dawn,
Yet coy as Aurora when over the hill top
  She peeps, is the face of my fair Colleen Bawn.

Her eye is the brightest, all nature confesses,
   And witching her glance as the light of the moon,
Like the floss of the maize are her soft silken tresses ;
   Her smile e'en Apollo would crave as a boon.

As boughsome her form as the breeze-bending willow ;
   More graceful her movements than those of a deer ;
Light-hearted and free as the foam-tossing billow ;
   This sweet little maiden has nowhere a peer.

In truth, of her sex she is worth quite a dozen,
   A fact that one running need scarce stop to see ;
And had not fate cruelly made her my cousin,
   A nearer relation she some day might be.

---

## MEMORIES OF MILLACOMA.

Millacoma is the Indian name for a river in Oregon.  Its poetical sound
may have influenced my imagination considerably in the  story which this
poem tells.  At all events, " Josie " is no clue whatever to the identity of
the person referred to.

Near Millacoma's mountain flood,
   My mem'ry often strays,
To revel 'neath the virgin wood,
   That shades its rugged ways ;
To think of times long since gone by,
   When hopeful, blithe and gay,
With winsome little Josie I
   Beguiled my hours away.

Its turgid, tossing, tireless tide,
   How oft with longing sigh
I've crossed, nor reck'd how swift or wide,
   With Josie in my eye ;

While on the quick'ning current sped,
  The boundless deep to swell;
I've lingered on the mossy mead,
  Where Josie used to dwell.

And there in quiet by the shore,
  I've sat while songbirds trilled,
And told the tale that oft before
  Less eager ears have filled;
But now from Millacoma's stream
  I've wandered far away;
And Josie of my youthful dream
  No longer holds the sway.

We loved—but time and distance both
  Conspired to conquer Fate;
And now, while I am nothing loth,
  She trusts a truer mate:
But still near Millacoma's flood
  My mem'ry often strays,
To revel 'neath its shady wood,
  And muse on other days.

## FANCY'S VAGARIES.

While in California I once met a pretty girl who was a very sweet singer.
Among the songs with which she used to charm me, I was particularly
delighted with her rendition of "The Fisherman and His Child," in the
chorus of which my readers will remember are the words "Come to me,
I love thee," supposed to be chanted by angels to a drowning boy.
After I first heard the song, it was several weeks before I could rid my
memory of the refrain; and to get even with the lovely creature whose
voice so haunted me, I wrote:—

  In the stilly hours of midnight,
    While upon my cot I lay,
  Dozing, dreaming, sighing, scheming,
    Sick at heart with life's affray;
  Through the dark and gloomy sadness
    Softly stole a voice I knew,

And in tones of melting sweetness,
  Came its message kind and true.
    "Come to me, I love thee,"
      Was the burden of refrain;
    "Come to me, I love thee,"
      Echo whispered back again.

It was Celia's voice enticing,
  That subdued my panting breast;
And I listened to its music,
  Soothed and wafted into rest.
From above I saw her smiling,
  And my sorrows all took wing;
While with melody beguiling,
  She was there, and Love, and Spring.
    "Come to me, I love thee,"
      Softly sounded in my ear;
    "Come to me, I love thee,"
      Softer still the accents dear.

Then her lips upon my forehead
  Tenderly the vision placed;
And she kissed me as I slumbered,
  With a touch so pure and chaste,
That my brain was bathed in perfume,
  And my soul in perfect bliss
Caught again the tender message,
  Chaster far than loving kiss:
    "Come to me, I love thee,"
      From afar the accents creep;
    "Come to me, I love thee,"
      Till I sank in sweetest sleep.

## WHILE I AM WITH CELIA.

How the winged moments fly !
Hours unnoticed pass me by ;
Time is but a round of joy ;
   While I am with Celia.

When in shine or shade we meet,
Thrills of pleasure, O how sweet !
Cause my heart to louder beat,
   While I am with Celia.

All forgotten is the care
That within my breast I bear ;
She alone is mistress there ;
   While I am with Celia.

When by Luna's light we walk,
'Witching rays around us flock ;
Till in raptures wild I talk,
   While I am with Celia.

With the purest, noblest zeal,
'Neath her gaze inspired I feel ;
And her smile is honor's seal,
   While I am with Celia.

I have sworn to be her friend,
And may God my vow defend ;
Perfect are the hours I spend,
   While I am with Celia.

May her days on earth be long ;
May she never know a wrong ;
And may life be one sweet song ;
   Is my wish for Celia.

## THE STORM-KING.

Outside the storm-king fumes and frets,
　　While streaks of fire flash from his eye ;
Against the pane a torrent beats,
　　And distant rumblings rend the sky.

But all oblivious of his wrath,
　　Nor heeding e'en the lightning's dart,
Within I sit and pledge my troth
　　To Celia, guardian of my heart.

To Celia, whom I've learned to love
　　Far better than all else beside ;
And who, imprompted from above,
　　Has promised soon to be my bride.

What wonder then that all forgot,
　　The wind bursts howling o'er the lea ?
What wonder that the skies can plot
　　Unheeded by my love and me ?

Though hurricanes should never cease,
　　Their fury I could long withstand,
And deem my lot a life of peace,
　　With Celia walking hand in hand.

————

## THE OLD, OLD STORY.

I know a lovely dark eyed girl,
With rosy cheeks and raven curl,
With juicy lips and teeth of pearl,
　　　　And dimpled chin distracting;
Whose smile sets ev'ry brain awhirl,
　　　　　　That comes in reach attracting

But yet for all her pretty face,
Her lithesome form and girlish grace,

"Fare thee well, but not forever...
 Though I cross the ranging main,
Love like ours no sea can sever, —
 We but part to meet again."

They are not worth describing space,
       Beside her charming manner ;
While virtues in her heart have place,
       That fly perfection's banner.

She has a voice divinely sweet,
That draws all creatures to her feet ;
And when she sings, e'en gods entreat,
       (While human eyes do glisten)
That she to them the joy will mete,
       Of being near to listen.

And this fair angel from on high
Is mine,—I know not how or why ;
She yielded to each yearning sigh,
       I made with vow unswerving ;
And now, most blest of mortals, I
       Feel least of all deserving.

But God be praised that e'er I met
This lovely laughing-eyed brunette ;
I'd die to earn her pleasure yet,
       And free her from all sorrow.
For her my sun shall rise and set
       On ev'ry coming morrow.

———

## THE LOVER'S FAREWELL.

Fare thee well, but not forever ;
  Though I cross the surging main,
Love like ours no sea can sever :
  We but part to meet again.

Fare thee well, and may our parting
  Like a beacon ever burn,
Telling not of news disheart'ning,
  But of hopeful, sweet return.

Fare thee well ; and when with sorrow
   Time hangs heavy o'er your head,
Think of me and that bright morrow,
   When we'll share life's shine and shade.

Fare thee well ; let no foreboding
   Steep your loving heart in gloom :
With thy trust my footsteps goading,
   I can conquer any doom.

Fare thee well ; and now, my darling,
   Let the tears we can't control
Wash away all doubts unsterling,
   And unite us soul to soul.

\*   \*   \*   \*   \*   \*   \*

Fare thee well, but not forever ;
   Though I cross the surging main,
Love like ours no sea can sever :
   We but part to meet again.

## I LINGER STILL.

I linger still, though Pleasure's smile
   Illumes the distant way ;
Her hitherto unfailing wile
   Has lost all power to sway.

I linger still, though Wisdom frowns,
   And urges me to go ;
Her stern advice I leave to clowns,
   While I embrace my woe.

I linger still, though from afar
   Ambition's voice I hear ;
Unmoved I view the guiding star
   Of many a former year.

I linger still, though Duty calls,
   In pleading tones, " come back ; "
A stronger force my feet enthralls,
   And blocks my homeward track.

I linger still, nor blame my choice,
   Nor break the pleasing chain ;
I've heard a tuneful siren's voice,
   And must perforce remain.

For Cupid, coming unaware,
   So works my wav'ring will,
That now, though heaven above despair,
   With Love I'll linger still.

## THAT IS ALL.

Only a package of letters,
   Entwined by a broken lace ;
Only a bundle of fetters,
   That bind to a pretty face ;
Only some tokens of friendship,
   That had warmed, with increase, into love ;
Only a bliss-burdened message,
   And the web that was weaving is wove.

Only a tenderest parting,
   With promises—ne'er to be filled ;
Only a teardrop starting,
   But ere it has fallen, chilled ;
Only a misunderstanding,—
   A blund'ring, cruel mistake ;
And yet, from pride still unbending,
   Two hearts are ready to break.

## THE JILTED MAID'S LAMENT.

Thou pale-faced moon, whose mournful light
   Steals rayless from the solemn sky,
List to a maiden's woful plight,—
   For thou alone must hear my sigh.

I was not always thus forlorn ;
   My days were once but rounds of joy ;
Life's scented rose showed no dread thorn,
   Nor did its gems hold base alloy.

My happy heart was light and free ;
   And like the birds in yonder glen,
I sang with merry honest glee,
   Nor dreamt of care, or grief, or pain.

But soon across my pleasant path
   A lover came with earnest eye,
To pledge to me undying troth,
   And steal my peace with lover's sigh.

For months upon his smile I dreamed,
   Like living act his vow appeared ;
His lightest word truth's model seemed ;
   His frown deep through my vitals seered.

But wo, alas ! my doting heart
   Was shattered by its only pride ;
For, tiring of Love's fancied dart,
   My idol flitted from my side.

Afar he roamed, nor turned again
   To see the wreck he left behind ;
While I must hide the killing pain,
   Nor show my grief to human kind.

So pale-faced moon, whose mournful light
   Steals rayless from the solemn sky,
Keep thou the secret of my plight,
   While void of hope I droop and die.

## SHE IS A LULU.

(Written by request of a friend whose best girl at the time, happened to
be called Lulu Howe.)

Sexton loved a pretty maiden,
  Who from him was far away ;
And his heart with grief was laden,
  That he could not nearer stay.

For she was a lovely creature,—
  Gentle as a summer breeze ;
Beauty shone on ev'ry feature,
  And her voice each ear could please.

And as Sexton thought about her,
  Love o'erflow'd his honest heart ;
And to be a likely suitor,
  He besought my erring art.

Glad to do my friend a favor,
  But afraid that I might fail,
I enquired, with trembling quaver,
  " What he wished me to detail."

" Tell the world," he answered proudly,
  " For it wants to know, I trow,
" That the girl I love's a Lulu,
  " And, what's more, a Lulu Howe."

---

## THE BREAKFAST BELL.

Written while residing on Bellevue Stock Ranch, Southern California.

In the early hours of morning,
  When the birds begin to sing ;
And the sun with flash-light warning
  Calls the busy bee to wing,

I am startled by a tapping
  On my chamber's bolted door,
While this song disturbs my napping,
  And cuts short a blissful snore :
      Georgie, the bell has rung for breakfast.
        Georgie, you're surely not in bed.
        Georgie, how can you lie so reckless?
        Georgie, get up, you sleepy head.

As I hear the merry summons,
  'Fore my eye there comes a face;
And I see the blushing features
  Of my charming little Grace.
And I doze again forgetful,
  Dreaming I'm in Paradise,
Till once more I hear the accents
  Of that fascinating voice, singing :
      Georgie, the bell has rung for breakfast.
        Georgie, you're surely not in bed.
        Georgie, how can you lie so reckless?
        Georgie, get up, you sleepy head.

All the peace that song engenders
  In my lone and aching heart,
I would fain—but nature hinders—
  To the world at large impart.
Oh how pleasant!  If forever
  O'er life's changing, troubled deep,
I could hear that voice enticing,
  Rousing me from morning sleep, singing :
      Georgie, the bell has rung for breakfast.
        Georgie, you're surely not in bed.
        Georgie, how can you lie so reckless?
        Georgie, get up, you sleepy head.

# A MAIDEN'S SONG.

While residing for a time in Southern California, I met my proverbial fate in the person of a beautiful little damsel whose first name was Grace. Neither attention nor poetry, however, could distract her thoughts from a certain gentleman some few hundred miles away, who, it appeared, struggled under the aristocratic cognomen of Clyde. In sheer desperation, therefore, I finally gave her this song to show my virtuous decision of submitting to the inevitable.

The hours flit past with merry speed ;
   The birds sing in the trees ;
The daisies bloom upon the mead,
   And scent the zephyr breeze.
But all too slowly time creeps on ;
   Unheard the songsters chide ;
For still I sigh from dawn to dawn
   To see my darling Clyde.

CHORUS.
My lovely Clyde, my manly Clyde,
   The idol of my heart ;
I long to nestle by his side,
   And never more to part.

A time there was when free as air
   I blithely sang of love ;
But now, entrapped in Cupid's snare,
   My thoughts such joy reprove.
Far from the darling of my choice
   The world seems wild and wide.
How can a love-sick maid rejoice
   When parted from her Clyde?

But I'll not brood upon my woes ;
   Nor rue my lot severe ;
For Time and Distance, present foes,
   Will give me back my dear.

H

Then let me dry my tear-stained face,
　　And true, whate'er betide,
I'll always be his loving Grace,
　　And he my darling Clyde.

———

## POOR DOLLY'S ILL.

The flowers grow parched in ev'ry glade,
In sympathy they droop and fade,
Their pretty peer is lowly laid ;
　　　　　　　Poor Dolly's ill.

The birds sing sad on ev'ry spray,
Untuned and broken is their lay ;
Each mournful accent seems to say,
　　　　　　　Our Dolly's ill.

The sun shines rayless from on high,
The wailing wind sweeps o'er the sky,
Time drags its dreary moments by,
　　　　　　　Since Dolly's ill.

All nature weeps, but weeps in vain,
Her master-piece still writhes in pain,
What art can make her glad again,
　　　　　　　While Dolly's ill?

(Later)
Once more the birds sing sweet and clear ;
The flowers once more their beauty wear ;
Once more all nature doffs her care ;
　　　　　　　For Dolly's well.

# WAS IT A PROOF?

Twas Autumn; and the wailing wind
   Foretold of Winter nigh,
As bleak and blind, it vainly pined
   To change the cheerless sky:
When with Zetulba by my side—
   Her hand, in promise, mine—
I craved (nor tried my doubts to hide)
   Of love some surer sign.

'Twas in a garden that we stood,—
   A plot her skill had made;
Where 'mong its flowers in musing mood
   She oftentimes had strayed.
But now its beds, of beauty shorn,
   Were dead, unkempt and bare;
What leaves were left shook all forlorn
   And desolate in air.

One only flower remained to tell
   Of garden glory fled;
A pansy—heedless of the knell
   That low its comrades laid.
Still fresh and sweet, it raised aloft
   Its bosom to the sky,
And dared the fates to show their hates—
   It simply *would* not die.

And as I pressed, with lover's zest,
   My darling's trembling hand;
And begged once more some token sure
   Of Cupid's magic wand;
She stooped—and though the season's last,
   Her garden's only plea—
She plucked that pansy from the waste,
   And handed it to me.

## A BACHELOR'S LEAP YEAR LAMENT.

Not married yet! Though years are flying by,
Not married yet! No wonder that I sigh.
Time still goes on, but in its fleeting train
Comes no sweet hope to cheer a lovesick swain.

Not married yet! And must I ever roam?
Not married yet! Oh, whither is my home?
When I was young I thought it wise to wait;
But now it seems I've waited till too late.

Not married yet! My aching heart repeats,
Not married yet! Nor tasted nuptial sweets.
Why is it thus? I constantly enquire;
And Echo's answer faint but whips my ire.

Not married yet! What can I—must I do?
Not married yet! Shall I but live and rue?
Where is the heart that heav'n cut out as mine?
Oh, tell me quick or let me life resign.

Not married yet! Still singly blest I rove.
Not married yet! No darling wife to love.
Come, wayward fair, while leap-year gives you choice,
With one short breath make my sad heart rejoice.

Not married yet! Though years are flying by.
Not married yet! No wonder that I sigh.
Time still goes on, but in its fleeting train
Comes no sweet hope to cheer a lovesick swain.

# Autograph Verses, Epigrams, Epitaphs, etc.

# ACROSTIC AND AUTOGRAPH VERSES.

### TO GRACE.

Gold is nothing but glittering dust,
Rubies at best are but stone,
All wealth is mere dross,
Cease pining its loss
Enjoy what you have without moan.

### TO ANNIE.

A woman who wishes to be
No laggard in beauty and grace
Need have no cause for fear,
If she will but keep clear
Each folly which tends to debase.

### TO LIZZIE.

Lizzie, if you wish to be happy
In this world of care and woe,
Zealously labor and try to be
Zephyrs to each friend you know,
Inasmuch as trying will help you
Equally happy with them to grow.

### TO EDIE HOWE.

Eagerly I took your album,
Dipped my pen deep down in ink,
In the meantime trying truly,
Ev'ry plan I could to think.

Here at last I make confession,
Oh! believe me, for 'tis true,
When each thought of line was written
Ev'ryone suggested you.

### TO GERTRUDE.

Goodly looks and graceful actions,
Each by virtue close entwined.
Reap respect from e'en the dullest,
Take the hearts of more refined.
Rate me pray amongst the latter,
Untold thoughts I can't appease,
Duty, Pleasure, I would forfeit
Eager much your grace to please.

### TO NELLIE.

Now that I have a chance to write
Each wish I have for thee,
Lest I should leave e'en one from sight
Life seemeth sad to me.
I therefore write with bated breath—
Each joy that's known be thine till death.

### ANOTHER.

Nearer to thee I feign would be,
Even in time of woe;
Long years with thee could only be
Long years of joy to know;
I therefore write this humble prayer,
Each hour give me that you can spare.

### TO MAGGIE.

Many friends in here have written
All professing they are true;
Greedy to admit they're smitten,
Gladly writing love to you;
If I thought my case not hopeless
Eagerly the same I'd do.

### TO EDNA (NICKNAMED "NED").

Each moment since I saw her face
Distracted here and there I've sped ;
Nor balm nor hope can peace replace,—
All life seems void apart from Ned.

---

### TO LEORA SHUMWAY.

Ladies, lilies, love and laughter,
Each admirers have if pure ;
Oft are zealously looked after,—
Reap respect from all is sure.

Ardently men sigh that women
Shall, when qualified, combine
Heaps of all the many virtues ;
Use has made th'above the sign.

Must I then, without inflation,
Write what I have thought of you ;
And I pen : " This combination
You possess if any do."

---

## HOW LIFE IS PUNCTUATED.

Life is but a page of sorrow,
Underscored with grief and woe ;
Leisure moments are its commas,
Used each breathing place to show ;
Hours of pleasure, like the periods,
Only here and there are found ;
While its days of bliss still scarcer,
E'en as paragraphs abound.

The above was written for my typewriter friend, C. W. S——, while I
was enjoying the felicity of a "Comma"; and is an acrostic on the name
of his best girl.

## TO EULALEE.

When years have flitted o'er my head,
   And I am old and gray ;
I'll often muse on years long fled,
   And of each one I'll say :

'Twas '67 when I was born
   To life and all its wants ;
In '71 one happy morn,
   They dressed me up in pants ;

In '73 I went to school,
   To learn my a b c ;
In '82 I left its rule,
   Quite tickled to be free ;

In '85 I fell in love
   With one, alas ! the day,
Who false in '88 did prove,
   And drove me far away ;

In '92——then there I'll wait,
   To chuckle in my glee,—
Why that's the year, by all that's great,
   I first met Eulalee !

---

## TO A CHANCE ACQUAINTANCE.

Dear Miss Cogher, though but seldom
   We have seen each other's face,
Yet I have been quite enamored
   Of thy beauty and thy grace.
And though Fortune be against us,
   And we never more should meet,
Yet with fondness I'll remember
   All our friendship, short but sweet.

TO ———— (IN MEMORY OF A GAME OF FORFEITS).

If there's aught that is better
Than diamonds or pearls,
'Tis plucking ripe cherries
With lovable girls.

---

### TO ETHEL.

Little Ethel, bright and fair,
Crowned by locks of golden hair,
With her eyes of roguish blue,
And her cheeks of rosy hue,
Has so gladdened me of late,
That I fain would bribe old Fate
To forget for once his laws,—
Banish from her life its flaws,
Make her years but rounds of pleasure,
Full of joy and health and leisure,
And when death at last must come,
May it whisper "welcome home."

---

### TO A LADY

With whom, while a member of the Vancouver *World* Staff, I used to
have many a discussion on Chinese immigration :—

If you wish to be happy, pray take my suggestion,
And get yourself right on the great Chinese question ;
Then when " justice to all" is your motto unfurled,
I know you'll remember the scribe of the *World*.

---

### TO CELIA.

'Twere useless, Celia, I confess,
To longer hide my love for you ;
Nor time, nor place can now impress
Another image on my view.

In waking hours your smiling face
 Inspires my thoughts with noblest themes,
And when I rest in sleep's embrace
 You are the angel of my dreams.

Your form is mirrored on my heart,
 To live away from you is pain ;
Sweet Celia, quick to me impart
 If I must love but love in vain.

---

### TO A YOUNG LADY

Who lived in a suburban town, and whom I used to see off on her train
quite frequently :—

When silver threads are mingled with
 Your golden locks of hair,
Perchance at whiles you'll take your specs
 And find this album rare.
You'll turn its pages one by one
 Till this vile scroll you gain ;
Then with a knowing smile you'll say :
 " That old three-thirty train."

---

### TO ANNIE.

When age and care have changed your hair
 To locks of snowy white ;
When time and tide, by youth defied,
 Have nearly dimmed your sight;

With tott'ring steps and flutt'ring heart,
 You'll find this book at times ;
And as you scan each Cupid's dart
 Well hid beneath these rhymes,

You'll pass some by with deep drawn sigh,
 At others you will chaff,
But when this page you chance to spy,
 You'll hold your sides and laugh.

### TO JESSIE.

I've fumbled o'er your album neat
   With many an anxious look ;
I've turned the leaves o'er one by one,
   Gazed into ev'ry nook ;
But truth to tell I've only found
   One full page in the book.

I therefore with prophetic pen
   To write its fortune dare ;
A few more years will soon have passed,
   Its leaves now white and bare
Will then be full of loved ones' names
   And autographs quite rare.

Each page will breathe some loving wish
   For you of untold bliss ;
Perchance at whiles you'll look them o'er
   With many a sigh and kiss;
And when you do, please don't forget
   To stop and sigh at this.

---

### TO LAURA.

When seas and rivers, vales and hills
   Divide me from fair Laura ;
Nor harp, nor bird with merry trills
   Can drive away my sorrow.

Where'er I roam, how near or far,
   Through scenes for grandeur peerless ;
If they remind me not of her,
   Alas ! they will be cheerless.

For Laura sprightly, sweet and pure,
   So full of love and duty ;
With tender eyes and face demure,
   To me is soul of beauty.

## TO PORTIA.

Golden rays of brightest sunshine
  Enter through the thickest cloud,
Roses often grow in splendor
  Where the coarsest weeds do crowd;
So it is with you, sweet Portia,
  In this world of sin and care
Both in features and in goodness
  You keep blooming fresh and fair.

———

## TO MARTHA MILLS.

Man indeed's a great creation,
  Ev'ryone admits 'tis so ;
And it needs no long creation
  To explain what all do know.

But despite his power and greatness
  And his large expansive mind,
For a peer, e'en though he's mateless,
  He need not go far to find.

Woman, yes, despotic woman,
  Makes him do whate'er she wills,
And much more if she's a charmer,
  Like my friend Miss Martha Mills.

———

## TO MAGGIE THORP.

When Juneau's mists and Juneau's hills
  Have faded from the scene,
And when 'tween me and Juneau's girls
  Vast oceans intervene ;
I'll feel so sorry, glum and sad,
  So wretched, lonely, blue ;
There's nothing sure will make me glad,
  But coming back to you.

### TO MRS. THORP.

At an Easter festival in Juneau, Alaska, a personified nursery rhyme performance was given, in which Mrs. Thorp's son Murph represented the personage who ministered to the *pious* wants of the author, supposed to be Simple Simon.

In after years, when looking o'er
 These leaves then tore and shattered,
While thinking of the friends who wrote
 Your praises true or flattered ;

Try hard to call to mind that night,
 When Murph was Tom the pieman ;
For then 'twill be an easy flight
 To think of Simple Simon.

### TO JIM THOMAS.

Whose lamp the author accidentally broke at an entertainment in North Bend, Oregon.

Dear Thomas, if the truth be spoken,
 You must be a sqrry scamp,
If your ties of love are broken
 Just as easy as your lamp.

## MISCELLANEOUS.

To *write all* your praises
 Seems to me so absurd ;
I think I'll just speak them,
 And not write a word.

When in a whirl of joy and glee
I care not if you think of me ;
But when you're sad and feeling glum,
Confide in me and I'll keep mum.

My love for you is like a tree
  In some green woodland dale,
As older it doth grow in years,
  It grows more strong and hale.

———

If all your praises I should write
  Within this little book,
I fear none else would have a page,
  Nor e'en one little nook.

———

I take your album off the shelf,
  And write above my name
These words, to show my love for you
  Will always be the same.

———

In after years when time and tide
  Have changed your hair and features,
You'll find this book, and laughing say :
  How oft I charmed these creatures.

———

As the air is full of birds,
So this book of gentle words ;
As the sea is full of fishes,
So this page of my good wishes.

———

When life is done, its troubles o'er,
May death be but the open door
Through which you'll pass to brighter shore,
To enjoy peace for evermore.

———

Though I feign would conceal what I'm forced to admit,
Since I saw you I've lost both my heart and my wit ;
For none else can I love ; nought else can I do,
But think, talk or sing of my meetings with you.

That there's many a slip 'twixt the cup and the lip,
  Is a proverb as old as it's true;
So when friends make a break, be quite certain you take
  The intention for all that they do.

---

Though the weeks of our friendship are scarcely a score,
  I feel, as I now say adieu,
That 'tis well for my heart we so quickly must part,
  Else soon 'twould be broken in two.

---

In haste I glance your album o'er,
  Then take my ink and pen,
And write this word or two to say,
  I hope we'll meet again.

---

## ON AN EMPLOYER

Whose most prominent trait was an ever-growing desire to be thoroughly understood. In his efforts to make his instructions plain, or, as he himself termed it, " self-explanatory," he had become very tautological in his style of composition, while his conversation fairly bristled with the interrogation, " do you understand ? "

Here Carr lies low ; Death's magic wand
Has proved its power, " you understand ? "
No more his wordy ways will worry,
For reasons " self explanatory "

---

## ON THE SICKNESS

Of one who for a time was my friend as well as foreman.

Good Lord, in pity pray look down,
  And save me from disaster ;
You know yourself I'll be a clown,
  If you do take my master.

I

## ON MY EARLIEST PATRON.

In sweet oblivion 'neath this tomb,
　　Friend Forbes lies in state ;
While ling'ring near in cheerless gloom,
　　We mourn our luckless fate.

For such a jovial fellow, he,
　　With ne'er a downcast face ;
Vain, vain the hope, all men agree,
　　To fill his vacant place.

-------

## TO A FRIEND WITH A WEDDING PRESENT.

Dear Tom, please accept this small gift from a friend,
For with it good wishes I also do send ;
May you be so well pleased with your wife and your lot,
That you'll never be sorry for " tying the knot."

May the pleasures of life o'er your pathway be spread,
And may long years of comfort roll over your head,
And when little Roseblades come round you to worry,
Call one of them after your friend Geo. G. Currie.

-------

## MODEST BUT SINCERE.

Though many men of many minds
　　Have raised their tuneful lyre,
And to its tune have courted fame
　　With poet's zeal and fire ;

Though they may choose the fitful muse
　　To make their lives seem brighter ;
I'll be content, with Fate's consent,
　　To be a short-hand writer.

## TO A LANDLADY ON HER BIRTHDAY.

May all your sorrows, cares and strife,
    And all your many troubles,
When close examined, prove to be
    But little empty bubbles.

Rejoice and sing with heartfelt glee
    Some pleasant joyous tune'
On this your yearly jubilee,
    The twenty-ninth of June.

And may you still with woman's skill
    Each boarder's life beguile ;
Nought makes them half so happy as
    The Missis' cheerful smile.

---

## LINES

Written on the back of a Perpetual Calendar and Almanac, Jan. 7th, '86.

This almanac will tell the time,
Long after I have ceased to rhyme.
But may I still be known to fame
When it no longer has a name.

---

## A BRAGGART'S EPITAPH.

Beneath this stone poor Horace lies
    In cold and silent death ;
He blew so hard when strong and well
    He used up all his breath.

## ON A WELL-KNOWN TOPER.

Dear friends, a line or two will do
    To tell you who lies here ;
For 'neath this stone, without a groan,
    There lies a keg of beer.

In other words, here lies T—P—,
    A victim to strong drink ;
To whisky's lair he went so near,
    He toppled o'er the brink.

---

## ON AN ELDERLY GENTLEMAN

Whose irritability made it impossible for those with whom he had to
deal to ever understand his quite frequently proffered instructions. When,
however, his orders were carried out apparently to the letter, it was the
most natural thing in the world to hear him say in anything but amiable
tones : "Look here, I told you from the first that that was wrong."

Death surely is a daring demon,
To brave the wrath of uncle Heman ;
And heedless hear his dying song :
"I told you, Death, that that was wrong."

---

## ON A VERY ESTIMABLE YOUNG LADY.

Tread lightly here, for 'neath this mound
    A lady fair doth lie ;
A fact which proves to all around,
    That saints do sometimes die.

In life so beautiful and good,
    Unerring and divine,
Perhaps 'twere better that she should
    Mid heaven's beauty shine.

## ANOTHER.

'Twere easy seen that will of man
    With Death has nought to do ;
For 'neath this stone poor Ida lies,
    While all the world doth rue.

In life so full of joyous fun,
    So beautiful and fair ;
When Death her person would not shun,
    What then will he not dare ?

---

## ON " THE ALLIANCE LIFEBOAT CREW,"

A temperance society, whose leading spirit or captain made off for
parts unknown with the hard-earned funds left in his charge by the young
organization.

Beneath this stone, in breathless sleep,
    The Lifeboat Crew doth lie ;
All those who wish may come and weep—
    'Twas want that made them die.

Their captain 'midst a passing storm
    Decamped with all their " tin ; "
And compassless left them to steer
    From out a sea of sin.

Quite manfully they tried to head
    Their leaking craft for shore ;
But all in vain their efforts proved,
    For soon they lost an oar.

They kept from swamping for a time
    Till mutiny arose ;
They then resign'd their lease of life,
    And turned up all their toes.

## ON A CHRISTMAS CARD TO A FORMER LANDLADY.

Though I'm far from Torrance Street
    And the friends that there reside,
Fortune holds my weary feet,
    And all homeward movements chide.

Yet I'm comforted by knowing
    That their friendship is no myth;
And a token of that knowledge
    Is this card to Mrs. Smith.

---

## ON A XMAS CARD TO JACK.

Here's to the friend I consider my best;
    Without him I fear I'd be lost, oh!
His worth I have often put hard to the test,
    By pressing him close in the Roscoe.

I like him because he is honest and true;
    Because by ill winds he's not tost, oh!
And because he is one of the well-favored few
    Belonging to famous old Roscoe.

Its Milligan upright and just that I mean;
    And when o'er his body shall moss grow;
High up on his tomb this one line should be seen:
    "Here lies the best man in the Roscoe."

---

## LINES

Written after reading Carlyle's "Heroes and Hero Worship."

To thee, oh God, this prayer I make;
Oh grant it for thine honor's sake:
For all my tasks and labors here,
Give me a will and heart sincere.

# WITH A PRESENT

To a lady in whose house I used to reside while in Lindsay, Ont.

If there's aught I dislike it is being ungrateful
　　For kind little offices strangers may do ;
So I think that it would be both heartless and hateful
　　To not own the debt that I owe Mrs. Trew.

When sick and in trouble, alone and dejected,
　　She ministered unto my every need ;
And showed to me kindness so little expected,
　　It cannot but make me feel grateful indeed.

Accept this small gift, Mrs. Trew, as a token,
　　To prove the confession above is sincere ;
And may it be pledge of a friendship unbroken,
　　To follow and bless us through each coming year.

---

# ON A XMAS CARD TO FATHER.

Christmas bells their chimes are ringing,
　　And the world, on pleasure bent,
Of its joys are loudly singing,
　　Filled with glee and merriment.

Voices mingling, sleighbells jingling,
　　Everywhere with gladsome sound ;
Hearts are lighter, hopes seem brighter,
　　Christmas has once more come round.

With this card and earnest greeting,
　　Full of filial wish from me,
Father dear, may Christmas lavish
　　Stores of joy and bliss on thee.

## ANOTHER.

Once again has Christmas season
   With its joy and bliss come round;
Once again the air is laden
   With a glad and happy sound.
Dearest father, may this find you
   Hearty, snug, and full of glee,
May it also help remind you
   Oftentimes to think of me.

---

## ON A LITTLE GIRL

Who just lived long enough to make herself sorely missed when
called by the stern reaper to " a better place."

Ye strangers here in wonder stand
And see the work of Death's dread hand ;
That awful power no more despise,
His latest victim Mary lies.
No fairer flower, no brighter gem
Could he to such a fate condemn,
And we the losers by Death's gain
Must give her up, despite the pain.

Her years, though barely half a score,
Have made her loss to us so sore,
We cannot still our throbbing hearts,
Now vacant left by fate's fell darts.
Those large dark eyes, that pretty face,
Must now enhance a better place.
From earth she's gone to realms above,
To taste the sweets of heavenly love.

## TO A FRIEND ON HIS 36TH BIRTHDAY.

To you, dear friend, I here extend
   My wishes kind and true ;
But as a friend, I can't pretend
   To say much good they'll do.

You now have reached that point in life
   Which laughs at foolish fears ;
That point which sages wise would call
   The noontide of your years.

And so I need not wish you'll be
   Exempt from Passion's sway ;
You sure won't step from Wisdom's knee,
   To follow Fashion's way.

But may you reach Ambition's height,
   That longed-for spot so dear,—
That niche o'er which such time is spent
   Through every passing year.

May Pleasure throw her mantle warm,
   In folds across thy back ;
So that in future coming years
   No care thy brain will wrack.

And when OLD AGE shall change thy hair
   To locks of flowing white ;
May life's long years of toil wear off,
   Till lost in peaceful night.

## ON THE BLANK LEAF OF A DIARY.

This book is a mirror whose leaves retain
Impressions received from my heart and brain ;
When other friends tire at my tale sincere,
I always am welcome to tell it here.

## TO A LADY TEACHER

In the Indian Mission School at Sitka, Alaska, on the eve of her
marriage to a friend of the author's, named Millmore.

Here's to the sly rascal, who, to suit his ambition,
Has with sorrow so stricken the folks at the Mission.
And long life to the lady he met to adore,
And at last to convert into Mrs. Millmore.

Not prepared to draw wrath from a man who could dare
To aspire to the love of a person so fair,
I conclude by foreseeing : no care shall annoy
Their mutual welfare through a long life of joy.

---

## WRITTEN BY REQUEST

Of a lady who, for attention to an acquaintance during sickness, was the
recipient from him of a dozen glasses and a poetical letter of gratitude.

If ever a lady had cause for elation,
I now have I say without hesitation ;
For having just tried my true pathway to climb
I'm honored with presents, kind wishes and rhyme.

Many thanks for your friendship and wishes so fair,
Nor mention my trifling attention and care ;
I did but my duty. to help make amends
For your being disabled so far from your friends.

And again many thanks for the g'asses so rare
(With which you have coupled those wishes so fair),
May each draught ever quaffed from each glass but be
A toast to your health and your prosperity.

## WITH A CHRISTMAS PRESENT

To a young lady usually known by the nickname of " Ned."

As Christmas was coming, it ran through my head
I ought to send something to dear little Ned.
But what could I send her? Ah! that made me shiver,
For gifts should be pleasing and plead for the giver.
I pondered and ponder'd on that fact intent,
Till sudden it struck me —I'll send her some scent,
So that when o'er presents she muses alone,
She'll mix up my mem'ry with Eau de Cologne.

---

## WITH A BIRTHDAY PRESENT OF SOME CALIFORNIA FLOWERS.

Dear Laura, to show the undying good wishes
That Cupid awakes in those caught in his meshes,
Let me hope that this day mid your life's many hours
May be like a rose in a garden of flowers.

---

## TO MISS KATE CLARKE

And Mrs. M. Riley of San Francisco, in memory of many kindnesses
these lines are inscribed by their grateful author.

I've wandered long both near and far,
On foot, on horse, by boat and car;
I've supped with ev'ry class and clan,
From highest state to lowest ban ;
But on my ever-varying round,
This wholesome truth I've always found,
To stranger guest there's nought so free
As Irish hospitality.

## ON A STOUT LADY,

Whose obesity was not her only distraction.

Here Austie lies, nor will she rise
  Till worms her carcase lighten,
And then Old Nick will have her quick,
  With fat his fire to brighten.

---

## MELANCHOLY MUSINGS.

Though Worth may seem much strength to lend,
On Fortune most our hopes depend.
Things of the moment are we all :
By chance we rise, or stand, or fall.

---

Let no tender feelings when battling with Passion
  Incline one to leave the grim monster half sped,
For us, if he rallies, he makes no concession
  But feasts on our vitals until we are dead.

---

The world is a wide barren waste,
  Full of misery, want and despair ;
Its inmates are travellers spent with unrest,
  For life is the burden they bear.

---

## A COUPLET

Handed to a confrère in a newspaper office who had facetiously passed an
exchange called "Knowledge" to me with instructions to get all I could
from it.

You are a generous man indeed,
To give away what most you need.

## LINES INSCRIBED

On a blank leaf in a set of Shakespeare's works presented as a parting gift to a friend.

If you would know your fellow-man,
Or close his helpmeet woman scan,
Here turn your gaze ; for in these books
Are shown the foibles, whims and crooks,
The good and ill, the hope and fear,
That through these lives of ours appear.
Bear well in mind what Shakespeare says,
And you will thank him all your days.

---

## ENGRAVED ON A MONUMENT.

Erected to the memory of my parents and brother by the surviving members of the family.

Here 'neath the sod, oblivious though we weep,
A father, mother, and a brother sleep ;
Nor blame nor question th' inevitable frost,
If all too quickly their comradeship was lost :
The mystery of death, who curiously would brave,
Must first their loved ones meet beyond the
                              silent grave.

---

## ON A STAMP ALBUM

Purchased from me as an accommodation by a friend.

DEAR HOLLOWAY,
        As through this world your way you push,
        May you be always just as flush,
        As when, with open ready hand,
        You helped your " broke " but honest friend,
                                    G. G. C.

## TO MR. AND MRS. MARKLEY,

With a 5 o'clock china tea service on the 20th anniversary of
their wedding.

For twenty years, through rain and shine,
　　And ev'ry sort of weather,
You've plodded up Life's steep incline,
　　And faced its foes together.

By word and deed you've sown good seed;
　　And now around you spreading,
The harvest lies for you to prize,
　　On this your china wedding.

May Peace and Plenty, sov'reign pair,
　　Still strive your lot to lighten;
May sunny smile of offspring fair
　　Your home life ever brighten.

And with this gift (which, you will see,
　　Quite selfishly was chosen)
Make many a rousing cup of tea,
　　And pledge your loving cousin.

---

## ON JACK McADAM,

An old-time office mate, who had a rascally habit of purloining my
eraser, pencil or pen, for the sake of getting me " wild," as he very suggest-
ively termed it.

Ye thieves and robbers bold, draw near,
　　And keep your faces calm;
Here lies a man you once held dear,
　　Poor Johnny Mac-a–Dam.

## EPITAPH ON JUNEAU'S MUSE.

An effusion, entirely local in its way, and not especially commendatory of a rival paper, having appeared in the Junean *Mining Record* once upon a time, the *Free Press*, as the unfortunate rival was called, in its next issue inserted the following : " Some men in their own minds think they were born with a poetical inspiration, but the world generally classes them as the d———st fools of the human race." On the supposition that no muse, however hardy, could survive such a blow as that, the following verses were immediately placed before the public :

Upon the lonely mountain side
  Fair Juneau's muse lies buried ;
Its soul has crossed that great divide
  O'er which we all are ferried.

Despite its youth, despite its vim,
  Despite its good intentions,
It was maligned to suit a whim
  And further man's contentions.

The *Free Press*, maddened by the truth
  The poor deceased was telling,
Tried hard to mime the witty youth,
  But failed, with envy swelling.

It straightway, moved by foul intent,
  With venom fell to swearing ;
Our muse, unable to resent,
  Grew stiff as any herring.

P.S—Take care, take care, ye brimstone sprites,
  You'll soon, alas ! be weeping ;
Our muse recovered from the bites—
  It was not dead, but sleeping.

## TO A YOUNG LADY

Who was confined to her room with a very bad attack of boils.

Of envious Fate these lines I write,
　　Nor care I for her favor;
She placed my loved one in a plight,
　　Nor reached a hand to save her.

The jealous hussy saw the bliss
　　I sipped from Celia's smiles;
And that same hour, to show her power,
　　She pestered her with boils.

But never mind, my day will come,—
　　Revenge is always double;
And when it does, how very rum,
　　If boils should be Fate's trouble.

## PROVIDENCE.

As Time's great cogs are slowly turning
　　And youthful hours are fleeting by,
The goals for which our hearts are yearning
　　Seem to retreat at ev'ry sigh.

And while, with hurried step pursuing,
　　Sometimes we stumble on our road,
Impatiently our ill luck rueing,—
　　Behold we find 'twas for our good.

Thus God our way is ever guiding,
　　And when we least believe Him near,
Lo, for our future bliss providing,
　　Mid dark despair His ends appear.

## ON MY FRIEND GRACE,

Whose most noticeable peculiarity was the very frequent ejaculation of the phrase, " Oh dear."

Poor Beauty runs life's dreary race
All lonely since we buried Grace ;
For 'neath this mound, a fettered guest,
The latter lies in dreamless rest.
Far up aloft on angel wing
Her soul has soared with saints to sing ;
But ere its flight, for parting cheer,
Sweet Echo caught one last " Oh dear."

---

## AN UNFORTUNATE'S LAMENT.

Alas ! Alas ! my case is sad indeed,
The thoughts of what I am would make a martyr bleed.
That I am lost unless I quick reform,
But makes me worse by heightening my alarm.
My conscience warns, but woe alas ! my will
Is powerless to act where passion leads me still.

---

## ON A CRAB SHELL,

Picked up on the shores of Alaska and taken to Cleveland, Ohio, by Dr. Volney McAlpine, a dentist of that city, whom I met while sojourning at Sitka.

Ye Cleveland strangers, hear my prayer,
And lift my corse with tender care ;
From Sitka's far off strand I've come,
Against my will, for 'twas my home.
Alive I scorned man's cunning wiles
And spurned alike his frowns or smiles ;
But when laid low by Death's dread stab,
Man picked me up a conquered crab.

K

## THE GRAVES OF A HOUSEHOLD.

This *gravely* prophetic composition was the result of an afternoon's compulsory confinement to my room at Lindsay, Ont., in the winter of 1888, owing to the woful prominence of a boil upon my face. The different epitaphs are for different members of the household in which I was residing at the time, and, of course, allude to peculiarities for which each was noted. Wright, whose obituary notice seems to require some little explanation, was an accomplished artist, besides being a professor of science and astronomy in Lindsay Collegiate Institute. It is hard to say whether this sample of character reading will be of any interest to people not acquainted with the originals, but I insert the poem here on account of its containing a record of my own fate ;—the author's epitaph in the eyes of many being a very appropriate *finale* to a book of poetry.

(1)    Ye gazing multitudes, surround
            This garden of the dead ;
       Stand and revere this spot of ground,
       Where tombs of mortals now abound,
            Who from base clay have fled.

       Beneath these costly sculptured stones,
            Which you do now behold,
       In silent death are laid the bones
       Of all that really now atones
            For the once Trew household.

(2)    Here lies in sweetest known repose
            The form of Mrs. Trew ;
       Why Death her form so quickly chose
       Not e'en a living mortal knows ;
            They only see and rue.

       A wife more true 'twere hard to find,
            So patient and so good ;
       And then as mother, oh so kind,
       E'en to a fault she oft was blind,
            Such love she bore her brood.

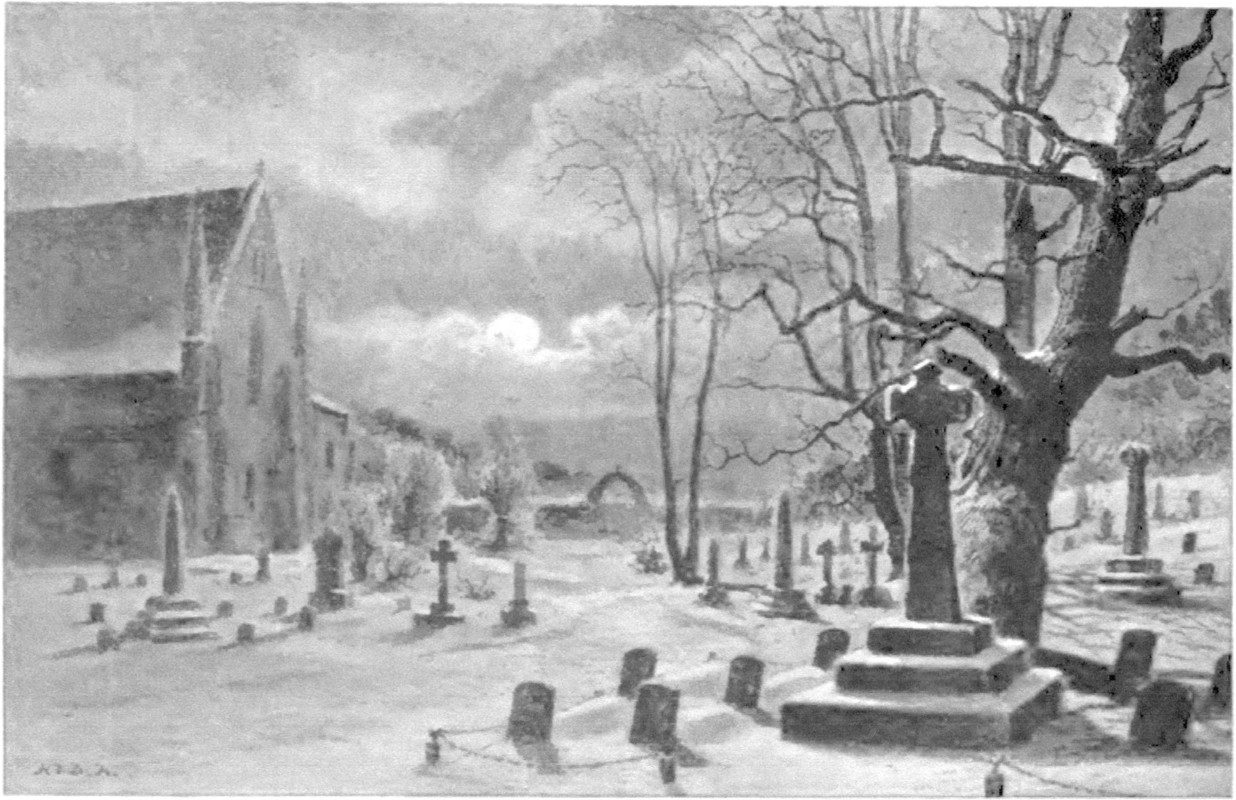

THE GRAVES OF A HOUSEHOLD.

A friend as true she also was,
    So tender, patient, wise;
A loss to all she'll be, because
In doing good she did not pause,
    Nor one did she despise.

(3)   Here lies his mould'ring spouse beside,
    A husband wise and good:
On earth, though few've been harder tried,
He kept the faith until he died,
    In philosophic mood.

But spite of trials hard and great,
    With jokes he did abound;
And with a countenance sedate,
Would oft some funny tale relate,
    To spread the laugh around.

With manner firm, and wise advice,
    And ever ready plan,
Within the home he was the spice,—
His worth was far above a price,—
    He was indeed a man.

(4)   Poor Harry 'neath this little mound
    Is laid away to rest;
Four feet or more of cheerless ground
    Now rises o'er his breast.

Had he but lived, a future age
    Might have revered his name;
But youth " repressed his noble rage "
    And barred the gates to fame.

An honest, thoughtful boy he was,
    A filial, duteous son;
We miss his earnest face, because
    Our hearts he early won.

(5)   Here Wilfred lies, some say brought low
        By making queer suggestions;
      But others think, who ought to know,
        He died from asking questions.

(6)   Ye fitful shadows, cease to play
      On this fast mould'ring human clay,
      "Twould suit you more to kneel and pray,
              Than that ye do.

      Ard you, vain, heedless mortals, stand!
      With awestruck face, view here the hand
      That could with ghastly features brand
              Poor Jack McHugh.

      He cared not when alive and well
      How many de (a) ers his victims fell;
      His voice too often was a knell
              None lived to rue.

      And yet his fellows found him brave;
      His friendship many men did crave,
      But now, alas! within this grave,
              Lies Jack McHugh.

(7)   Ye stricken creatures, cease your wailing,
      While I to others am detailing,
      How Death found out poor Burton's failing,
              And used it sore.

      To concert halls he went so often,
      A *program* e'en his brain would soften;
      So Death pinned one inside a coffin,
              And raised the door.

      And as poor Burton that way passed,
      Upon that bill one look he cast,
      But little thought it was his last,
              As near he drew.

Inside the box he quickly stept,
When down the lid behind him crept,
And soon in Death's cold arms he slept,
    While all doth rue.

(8)  Below in crisp and cheerless garb,
    Poor Wright in silence lies;
While o'er him grows an uncalled herb
    In hopes its name will rise.

Around his grave with doleful look,
    Are pebbles, rocks and stones ;
Collected there since life forsook
    His fast decaying bones.

And well they may their sorrow show,
    For did he not, while well,
With learned look and conscious glow,
    Their names and species tell?

How great, ye flowers and trees around,
    Must be your grief this day ;
'Twas he who did, with skillful art,
    Your very life portray.

And you, ye stars, in pity weep,
    For this your comrade dead ;
Who now will tell, profound and deep,
    The way your course is sped ?

And last of all, ye human race,
    With noiseless step draw nigh ;
When Death such learnedness can face,
    You sure have cause to sigh !

(9)  This stone was erected
    To recall that great person,
Who was known to this world,
    By the name of McPherson.

His holy demeanor,—
  Personified truth—
Has been used ever since
  As a guidance for youth.

How his wondrous career
  On this earth was begun
Is a myst'ry to most,
  And remembered by none.

But more wondrous his ending,
  If history's true ;
For in broadest daylight,
  He just faded from view.


(10)  And now to Cosgrove's tomb we come ;
      We gaze, but sorrow keeps us dumb :
      For it was he, our learned parson,
      Who taught us to translate Upharsin ;
      Who oft explained the gospel story,
      By parable or allegory ;
      And who in feeling tones did often
      Tell us how best to cheat the coffin.
      But here, alas !—his latest sermon—
      He lies the feast of hungry vermin.
      Ye gods, we humbly you beseech,
      O ! send him back, if but to preach.


(11)  Come here, aspiring youth, and learn
        What weapon Death will use,
      When he thinks fit to overturn
        A follower of the Muse.
      Poor rhyming Currie chanced to cross
        His pathway cold and bleak ;
      He straightway aimed, and felled him with
        A boil upon his cheek.

*9 7 8 3 7 4 4 7 6 7 2 6 2 *